This book is dedicated to my wonderful wife, Yvonne, who always believes in and supports me.

Table of Contents

Chapter 1

The tiny craft lay in quiet waters about a mile offshore as the neophyte sailors aboard studied the lay of the land and watched for any activity.

"According to the map, Leetra should be the first island." Idiptu crouched with his hands in front of him, placing the map on his lap. "Like we said before, this would not be a good choice for a rest. Leetra and Akadon nearly touch on the northeast side of this island. Most of the smaller islands are close by. However, Afeena is still a good distance away, so that is probably where the Farragon sailed from."

Mashua sat next to him and looked back and forth between the map and the island. "But I see little difference in the south side of any of these islands. Suppose we missed our target and this is really Afeena? We leave here and head for open sea!"

Idiptu pointed at a little spot on the map. "See this little island? If we were looking at Afeena, we would be right on top of it." He moved his finger southwest. "See this one? If this were Akadon, we would probably be able to see this other little island as well. But I can say with some certainty; this island is not Afeena. We would do well to steer clear."

"But some of the other maps don't even show the smaller islands," Anam pointed out. "What if they are actually underwater or this map is totally incorrect?"

"I don't know." Idiptu shrugged his shoulders. "This is the best map. I'm betting on this one."

Marcis, another Denarite, snapped at Idiptu. "Look, if this really is Leetra, that means Afeena is still another whole day away. We're tired and hungry. I think we should go ashore anyway." Marcis had not yet grown close to God and still had his youthful short temper.

Idiptu glanced at Anam and folded up his map. "I'm not in charge here. I just navigate and advise."

The travelers had left Ifintim with enough food and fresh water for a seven-day journey. This had been after a considerable amount of discussion as Mashua had been convinced the Lord would ensure they would make it in three days. That had been ten hot days ago. Their seafaring inexperience and tiny craft had slowed them greatly. They had been extremely fortunate in finding the maps, and Idiptu had spent the last year studying maps, stars, and weather. Having no teacher, the progress had been difficult. Now, however, he was very pleased with himself. Regardless which of the three islands they had truly sighted, he had led them into a vast, empty sea and delivered them to the Isles.

"I think," said Anam, "we should go ashore. It is late in the day, and we have seen no activity there so far. We should go in and at least get some fresh water. We'll leave early tomorrow before we're noticed. Is there any argument to this?"

He looked over his crew. Mashua and Idiptu were now standing before him and merely shrugged their shoulders. Paluqua, Zoana, and Crazon were huddled together at the opposite end of the boat, speaking quietly among themselves. Marcis and Ahohiel sat on the roof of their little shelter, too tired to move.

"I see no reason why we shouldn't go ashore now," said Mashua. "Let's turn this thing around."

"Let's pray first," said Zoana, beckoning the men to join them.

As there wasn't room for everyone to sit in a circle, Mashua and Anam sat to one side.

"Sweet Lord," Zoana began, "we thank you from our hearts for delivering us across the sea to these new lands. You have sustained us sufficiently. You were kind in protecting us from the foul weather. Thank you for guiding the inexperienced hands of the builders in making a sure craft. Thank you for the wisdom you have given Idiptu in taking seemingly senseless things in the sky and bringing us to the threshold of these strange lands. Strange to us, my Lord, but not to you as you fashioned them and rule over the people here. Now, we don't know the future, but you do as you have already created it as well. Let us continue to be in your will, Father. We are, like this tiny boat, Lord, merely vessels in a vast sea, and we lean on you."

Mashua added, "God, we ask you to continue to watch over us. Tell us if our decision to go ashore is good with you or foolhardy." He immediately arose and began turning the sail and retying the cords.

The light breeze seemed ideal, for as soon as the sail was set, the boat turned and briskly moved toward the beach, which was flat and sandy. However, a few paces from the water's edge, it climbed swiftly into a rocky cliffside, punctuated by several crevices and caves.

At first, it was difficult for the travelers to move about on land, having been in the water for so many days. However, as soon as they were able, the boat was carried into an enclosure and tied securely. Then, they began a search for food and fresh water. Their roving soon brought them to a rather spacious cave, which opened right onto the water, creating an advantage of being fairly inaccessible to anyone snooping about. There was a small stream of fresh water running through the back end of it. The floor was flat and provided plenty of sleeping space. Driftwood was gathered to prepare a small fire after dark. Unfortunately, the mostly barren beach provided no source of food. They were able to catch a few fish, and these were roasted over the fire.

Soon after sunset, the tired crew began to drift into a sound sleep; the deepest in several days. Zoana was posted as the first guard. Around midnight she woke Marcis to relieve her. The back of the cave provided an ideal lookout as there was a small promontory making it possible to see everyone else, as well as the cave entrance. Behind the small natural seat ran the tiny brook of fresh water, which plummeted several feet into a deep chasm of darkness. The fire had been built near the entrance to keep out any unwanted animals.

"You have a good sleep, Zoana," Marcis said as she climbed down to her bedroll. She smiled and winked at him silently so as not to disturb the others, laid down, and immediately fell to sleep.

Unfortunately, Marcis soon passed into an uneasy slumber as well. It was not too easy to sleep on the perch without falling over, but due to his great fatigue, he did pass out.

Mashua slept closest to the fire and awoke much later to hear a hissing sound. The light of the fire was casting wildly dancing shapes onto the walls. It took a moment for him to realize the fire was acting so crazy because the tide had come in and was already up to the fire pit. He realized in another moment the fire would go out, so plunging his hand into the flames, he extracted the largest firebrand he could, just as the water lapped over the last of the flames and smothered the fire.

"Everyone up quickly!" he bellowed. "The tide has come in!"

By now, the water had reached him and soaked his bed-roll. A great deal of activity began to happen. Mashua held his torch up near the entrance, which was quickly becoming submerged in the rising water. Everyone began scurrying around to gather their belongings.

"Forget it!" he called out. "It's too late. We've got to get out of here now."

Marcis was the last to respond. When he realized what had happened, he leaped to his feet and quickly began to climb down. Then, he remembered his belt with his canteen and knife and dashed back up to get them, forgetting the dangerous dropoff. As he reached for the belt, he slipped and dove over the edge, screaming as he fell. He disappeared into the darkness. Most of the others had already made their escape by the light of Mashua's burning brand. When Mashua saw Marcis fall, he quickly moved toward the rear of the cave. As he ran up the slope, he slipped and dropped his torch, plunging himself and the few others who were still in the cave into darkness. By now the water had nearly reached the edge of the chasm. Terrified of falling as well, he slowly made his way to the edge and called several times for Marcis.

Zoana had left the cave when the warning was made but returned as her husband took so long to make his retreat.

"Mashua!" she screamed into the darkness. "Mashua, you have to get out of here. Are you there?"

"Yes," he said meekly, too quiet for her to hear. By now the sea water had begun to spill over the ledge. In a few moments the force of the water would be so great he would be washed away. With a heavy heart, he followed Zoana's voice to the entrance and held her hand as she guided him out.

Outside, they had all climbed to place a few feet above the now submerged cave entrance. The full moon was a blessing as it provided plenty of light to see.

"How could we all be so foolish?" Anam asked as Zoana and Mashua approached him and the others. He glanced around. "Where is Marcis?"

Shortly after the sun began to make its appearance, the water began to recede. When it was possible, they climbed down from their perch and investigated the cave. All their belongings were gone, having been washed over the ledge or into the sea. Mashua sat for some time, staring into the darkness.

Zoana came and sat beside him. "I just can't believe he's gone," Mashua said, shaking his head. "It was so odd. He just disappeared."

"Beloved," Zoana coaxed him, "it's time to go. We have found the boat and it is in fine shape. Everything else is gone. Anam wants to get away from the island before we are discovered. We prayed for a good reception at Afeena. Please, let us go now." She led him outside where they had readied the boat.

As he passed Idiptu, he commented, "You were right. We should have listened to you and not come ashore. Marcis messed up."

Anam took Mashua's hand and helped him into the boat. "Please, don't dwell upon it like this. There's nothing to be gained. Let's just concentrate on getting to Afeena."

Chapter 2

Marcis opened his eyes and winced as he gazed directly into the sun. A man was standing over him. "Who are you? How did I get here?" He tried to stretch out and could not as it caused too much pain. He realized he was lying in a brook. "I remember falling and nothing more."

"My person is of no matter to you. I am not an enemy. You were washed out into this culvert where I found you. You cannot move as you have broken several bones and ruptured some internal organs. However, you should thank God you are alive. You will mend."

"Are you a native here?" Marcis tried to focus on the other man's appearance, but due to the pain in his head and the glare of the sun, all he could see was a dark form.

"I am a worker here. My home is far away."

"Then," said Marcis as he propped himself up on one elbow, "since you are a worker here, can you take me to your boss? Perhaps he can help me."

The stranger laughed. "He can certainly help you. However, you are in no shape to come before him just yet."

"Then what will you do with me?"

"I will take you to the home of some people who will care for you." So saying, the man stooped down and easily lifted Marcis up. Marcis screamed from the tremendous pain and blacked out again.

"He's coming around, Mama! Come and see."

Marcis opened his eyes to see he was in a little farm-house. A young girl stood by him with a wet cloth. Outside, he could hear the bleating of sheep and the cackle of chick-ens. It took Marcis aback to hear her dialect of the Denarite tongue. For the past year they had, by agreement, been using almost entirely the cultural language that Mehi had begun to teach them before he died. It had become the common tongue of the Denarites and Rasomites. However, Anam and some of the women had also begun learning the Denarite lan-guage.

A portly woman came in from outside. There seemed nothing at all lovely about her. She wiped her dirty hands on her apron and pushed her greasy hair behind her ears. Her bare arms were as covered with patchy sores as was her face. When she saw Marcis look at her and attempt a smile, she grinned. Several teeth were missing, and the few remaining were stained yellow. Sitting next to him, she placed her hand on his forehead.

"Well," she said, "I wasn't sure there for a while, but I guess you'll survive."

It was then Marcis realized both his arms and legs were splinted and tied down. He glanced at the bonds on one of his arms. The woman pulled a knife from her apron pocket and stood over him. For a moment, he was terrified as she glanced up and down at his body and at the knife. When she saw his terrified expression, she chuckled and began cutting the ropes tying him down.

"Now do you think I'd spend a whole week nursemaid-ing you for some kind of sacrifice? You have had one wild week, my friend."

"Uh, my name is Marcis. Can you tell me what has happened? Did you put these splints on me?"

"Oh, yes, dear." She sat down by him again, having cut all the bonds. "A week ago today, me and Shelley," the little girl waved, "were sitting here eating and there came a knock at the door. Scared the daylights out of both of us. We get no visitors out here and had heard no one outside. Besides, the animals usually start a commotion if someone does show up. I opened the door and found you lying on the porch. I thought you were stone dead. I know you didn't knock on the door."

"There was another man. A man found me and said he was bringing me here. You didn't see him?"

"Nope. No one except you. Shelley," she looked at the girl. "Would you please get Marcis a drink?" The girl ran off and returned with a metal cup full of water which she helped him to drink from. "Anyway, somehow we lugged you to the bed and patched you up. It was easy setting the broken bones. I've doctored animals all my life. I just hoped you'd lay still and heal, but you had some wild nights when the fever hit, so we had to tie you down." She laughed out loud. "Never had a man tied to my bed before." Marcis laughed also.

"So, is it just you two out here all alone?"

"Yup. Just me and Shelley. My name's Roda. Husband died a long time ago, so we don't run the farm no more. I just keep the animals and a garden. Now, I don't mean to pry too much, but it doesn't sound like you're from Leetra or any of the other islands. Could you fill me in a little?"

"So, we are on Leetra. And Coracus? Is he still in charge of Leetra and Akadon? And a man called John Dunley?"

"Coracus runs all the islands. Life on Afeena is the worst. Most any resistance he had is either dead or locked away. As far as I know, John Dunley was killed in a battle at sea."

"Well, I may as well be honest and tell you everything. I can't defend myself, so I am completely at your mercy." He proceeded to tell her the story of his life in the cave, their eventual liberty, and especially, about the Rasomites. Finally, he told her how he had fallen during high tide and his rescue by the stranger. She stopped him many times to ask questions. In the meantime, Shelley had fixed a large salad and prepared a dessert of fresh strawberries and cream. When he finally was finished, she began to feed him, as he still could not feed himself.

"Well," said Roda as she stood up, "it's getting late and I need to take care of the animals. It's a very interesting story, and I feel bad for your friends. Won't make any difference what island they go to; the vermin will sweep down upon them. Their best plan would be to turn back to Ifintim."

"Well, I am afraid they have arrived at Afeena a long time ago. I wish there were a way I could know how they're doing. I'm not too worried, though. Anyone who would choose a Rasomite for an enemy is flirting with death."

"I hope you're right. Now you get some sleep. Shelley," she called out. "You fix something for Marcis that will put him back to sleep for a while. I'm going outside."

Chapter 3

After the loss of Marcis, the travelers had sped to Afeena, believing it to still be a free island. The winds had been favorable that day, and it was sighted early in the evening. They
could see towns and villages quite plainly on the south side
of the island, and they made a nearly complete circle about it,
finally finding a deserted beach on the northwest corner,
which they approached after dark. The Lord had protected
them from detection so they could travel the entire length of
the Isles.

Once ashore, the boat had been moved inland a considerable distance and hidden in a thicket of shrubs. As this corner
of the island was deserted, they made their camp on a
riverbank near the beach and began seeking food which was
found in abundance.

On the morning after their arrival, they had a meeting to
determine their next action. Ahohiel and Idiptu volunteered
to scout out the territory. It was obvious the Rasomites could
not do so anonymously. Therefore, soon after breakfast, they
departed.

They moved upriver and hadn't traveled far when they
came upon a village. Hiding themselves in the trees outside
of town, they waited for some opportunity to arise. Toward
noon, as nothing had presented itself, they bravely walked into town.

They found a neat little village of only a few hundred people. The homes around the outside of the village were all the same basic structure of cobblestone with thatched roofs. There were women working in their yards and a few young children. Other than a few casual stares, no one disturbed them.

After passing a few houses, one lovely young woman standing near her backyard fence, carrying a platter, spoke to them. "Good day, gentlemen, would you be interested in some cookies?"

They glanced at each other and smiled.

"Why certainly, my lady," said Idiptu as the two men approached her. They ate several of the small delicacies before speaking again.

"It's a hot day, isn't it, madam?" Ahohiel asked casually to make conversation.

"I suppose it is, master. But is it the weather you'd want to visit about? Will you be going into the house?"

The men glanced at each other and shrugged their shoulders.

"Do you have any children, madam?" Ahohiel asked casually to make conversation.

The woman's mouth fell open and she nervously shook her head. "Oh, no, sir! You have all my children. There are only the two boys. Please, don't take anything else." She nearly upset her tray of cookies.

Ahohiel helped her steady her tray. "Madam, I believe our intentions are completely misunderstood. We mean you no harm."

"Then if you are not informers are you escaped prisoners?"

"We are…" Ahohiel began.

Idiptu had a hunch and suddenly cut him off. "Yes, we escaped from Akadon and, uh, once lived on one of the other islands but feared returning. We fled here. Can you hide us?"

Ahohiel started to correct him but realized what he was doing.

"Then why are you hanging about in broad daylight if you are escapees?" she asked.

"We had hoped to blend into the community," Ahohiel joined in, "but you have figured us out." He looked at Idiptu. "We should get out of sight. This isn't going to be easy like we thought with no men around."

The woman glanced up and down the street and realized several neighbors were watching but could not have heard. She suddenly burst into tears and called out, "Then I am ruined! Yes, if you must, go and search the house." She led them to a gate and looked across the street to another woman who stood holding her hand over her mouth. "Hurry," she whispered, "I believe the trick is working." She led them inside.

The men were stunned by the barrenness of the interior. There was no furniture of any type. Two rooms were completely stripped. The first room, the kitchen, had a small wood stove and three shelves attached to the wall, upon which sat a minimum of staples and a few pots and pans.

"Is this how Coracus has left you?" asked Ahohiel.

She quietly nodded. "His informers and the local commander have taken everything."

"You mentioned two boys. Do you also have a husband?" he asked.

She watched them for a minute to ensure she could trust them, then nodded her head. "We had two sons. They would be nearly teenagers now. My husband is also a prisoner or slave and they tell me he is on Akadon. Perhaps you knew him. His name is Vylon." They shook their heads. "Oh, what I would do to see him again." She seemed very distant as she thought of her family, then seemed to snap out of it. "What island are you from?"

"Uh, we'd rather not say," said Idiptu. "I'm sure you understand."

"Oh, certainly." She glanced at her little food supply and back at them. "You must be very tired and hungry. As you can see, I have no bed or chair, but you are free to make yourselves as comfortable as possible. I want to feed you something. I had a little flour and sugar, so I made the cookies to bribe the informers if I needed to. It's best to act friendly. I can fix some soup, but I must go to my neighbor for a piece of meat."

The two men attempted to convince her it wasn't necessary, but she was determined and finally left, promising to return soon.

After she left, Ahohiel asked Idiptu, "Are we going to tell her the truth? I have a real bad feeling about all of this."

"Why? What's the problem? She thinks we escaped from Akadon where her husband is. We need her help." Idiptu was very insistent. "We need to play this for all it's worth."

Ahohiel paced about the empty home nervously. "We need to tell her who we really are and just trust God," he said.

"I trust God, but right now we have her support and we shouldn't change our story."

Ahohiel went to the front window and looked out. A few paces down the street the woman was returning to the house. Behind her were two large armed guards.

"We are betrayed!" he yelled as he ran to the back door. It was locked.

Idiptu stood in the middle of the room, watching his friend struggle with the door. They heard the latch lift on the front door. Ahohiel stepped back, ran, and rolled himself into a ball as he flew through the air, shattering the window.

"Stop them!" a voice yelled from behind him. He ran.

Idiptu was not so fortunate. He was quickly bound and gagged. One of the guards attempted to chase down Ahohiel, but his heavy weapons impeded his movements, and he soon gave up and returned to the house.

"You will help me, please!" the woman pleaded with the two guards.

"You have done very good, Estella," one of the guards said. "We will definitely put in a good word with the commander. I am certain he will want to interview you, and you can ask for his help."

Idiptu stood, quietly listening until he was led away.

A few minutes later, he stood before the local village commander. One of the guards briefly reported what the woman had told him concerning the two escapees. He ensured the commander that a search was already on for the one who was missing. The Commander instructed Idiptu be allowed to speak.

"What have you to say for yourself?" the Commander demanded. Then, in a calmer tone, "If you are honest with me, I may go easier on you. Are you, in fact, escaped from Akadon?"

Idiptu had been thinking since his capture of how he would explain himself. He was afraid to continue the lie as, if they began asking too many questions, they would know he was untrue. However, he was afraid to tell the truth and endanger the others. He finally decided to hold his secret a bit longer.

"I was a servant with my friend on Akadon. An opportunity arose for us to escape here. I heard the commander here was a compassionate man and would show mercy."

"Your name?"

"My name is Idiptu."

"Your dialect and name are very strange. Where will your friend go?"

"I don't know. I suppose he will attempt to hide out in the woods."

"Let me explain a few things!" he snapped. "First, if your partner stays on Afeena, he is an idiot. He will soon be captured. Second, I do not believe your story. There is something very odd about you. Lastly, I do not know from whom you heard you would receive mercy here, but we shall correct that fallacy right now." He pulled a short whip from his belt.

The guard shoved Idiptu to the ground.

Suddenly, Idiptu called out, "See that you do not do it, sir! To beat me could prove to be the gravest mistake of your life." The Commander stepped back and hesitated. "To save your life, you should put away your childish toy."

"Who are you?" he demanded.

Idiptu stood up and brushed himself off. "I have nothing to say to you. However, you had better treat my partner, as you call him, with care. You will be held directly accountable if he is harmed and our mission jeopardized."

"What mission?" By now the Commander was at once angry and afraid.

"I have already told you too much. I will tell you this. Our mission is ordered from the highest level, and our protector will deal directly with anyone offending us or our mission."

"Are you spies for Coracus?"

"I can tell you no more."

The Commander pulled his guard aside and told him to quickly call off the search until this could be better understood. When they were alone, he stood meekly before Idiptu.

"I had no way of knowing. You said nothing. You wear no insignia. What could I do? You said you had escaped from Akadon, so how was I to know?"

He prepared to continue his pleading, but Idiptu motioned for him to stop. He calmly closed his eyes and thought how amazing it was he had taken control so easily. Saying a silent prayer of gratefulness, he smiled at the Commander.

"That's enough of all this talk. It is now long after noon, and I have not eaten. It is your duty to be hospitable."

"Of course," he said. "Come with me."

A few minutes later, he sat at the Commander's own dining room table, eating and drinking sumptuously. His only concern was for his friends, whom he continued to pray for.

Chapter 4

When Ahohiel fled the woman's home, he had not gone far. Assuming his pursuers would head into the heavily forested area surrounding the hamlet, he had run a few paces and scurried into what appeared to be a seldomly used barn. Once inside, he realized it was a tool shed. His eyes gleamed at the machetes and other equipment as he thought of how he could use them for protection. He decided against it, however. He was neither a violent man nor a thief, so he stooped to his knees.

"Lord, thank you for that daring escape. Please, watch over my brother Idiptu. Also, I am sorry for any damage I caused to that lady's home. I know she betrayed us to help earn her family back. I hope she succeeds, but please, not at our expense. God," he took a deep breath, "I am really frightened. I feel now I can trust no one except my comrade and you, Lord. So, I put myself in your hands."

He heard a noise at the door and jerked his head up in fear. A little girl was staring at him.

"Are you hurt?" she asked.

He shook his head.

"Then why are you on the floor?"

"I was, uh, praying." He stood up. "Did you see me come in here?" She nodded. "Did anyone else see?" She shook her head. "Can you keep it a secret?" She nodded again. He breathed a sigh of relief. "What is your name?"

"My name is Lora." She curtsied and Ahohiel smiled.

"How old are you?"

"I am five years old, and my name is Lora." She curtsied again.

"You are a good girl, Lora. You must not tell anyone I am here."

"Are you going to surprise someone?"

Ahohiel looked into her innocent little blue eyes and smiled. He thought briefly of his mission and knew he could tell her the truth. "Yes, I am going to surprise someone, so don't tell anyone or the surprise will be ruined."

"You can have this for your house, and I won't tell anyone. Just a second." She turned and left.

A few minutes later she returned with a jar of cold water almost too big for her to carry. Ahohiel took it from her and swallowed a little. He opened his mouth to thank her, but she left again. A few minutes later she was back with a bowl containing crackers and cherries. Though he was very hungry, he politely ate one of the cherries and placed the pit in the bowl.

"Do you like berries?" she asked.

"Oh yes, I like berries. The cherries are very good. Thank you."

"Well, I have to go now, so goodbye." She surprised him by offering him a hug, which he accepted, and she ran off.

"The innocence of children," he said quietly. "Thank you, God."

That evening, back at the camp, the rest of the travelers were growing increasingly nervous at the tardiness of Idiptu and Ahohiel. As the sun crept lower toward the horizon, they began to give up hope of their return that day.

"Tomorrow, I shall sneak into the village and see if I can locate them," said Mashua as they settled in.

"And then you may disappear," said Zoana. "I don't like this sneaking around. We've never done this before. Normally, we just walk in and let them have it."

Anam laughed. "This is my old Zoana. And is this what God has said to you?"

"He has been silent. It's just my attitude that we are always vindicated when we are bold. Normally, one of us will go ahead and, after a little ruckus, the rest will show up. It all seems to work out in the end. We've never sent people in as spies before."

"Then," said Mashua as he flexed his muscles, "I will take your advice. Tomorrow, we shall start over. I will not go in as a spy, but I shall go boldly. Then, after I start a bunch of trouble, the rest of you can arrive."

Zoana shook her head and looked away from the rest. Paluqua and Crazon were praying together. Anam sat over the fire, staring into the flame in deep thought. Mashua was rolling himself into a ball and was prepared to go to sleep. They had no bedrolls, no extra clothing, nor many supplies, as nearly everything had been lost their first night in the cave. Most of their weapons had also been lost. However, they were grateful to have escaped with their lives, though saddened over the loss of young Marcis.

Zoana looked back at Mashua. "I am really distressed over what could have happened to Idiptu and Ahohiel."

Mashua motioned for her to join him. He kissed her on the cheek. "Please, don't worry. Tomorrow I will go in and straighten this out. You know they are full of faith, but sometimes they're simply not bold enough. I'm sure if they had used God's authority, like you said, things would have gone much better."

Mashua stood behind a tree very close to where Ahohiel and Idiptu had hidden the previous day. From where he stood, he could see most of the village. It was a quaint little village that had seen better times. Shutters hung ajar, weeds grew up in the yards, and he had seen one armed guard. However, he had seen no other men and only a few children. A few of them seemed to be dressed fairly well, but mostly their clothes were tatters. He was reminded of his raggedy clothes worn most of his life while in the cave. It seemed all the women were working in their gardens; some of which were adjacent between yards. But even when they were working together, they seldom spoke. It became clear to him that Afeena was no longer free, and the men had been taken away.

After a few minutes of contemplating this scene, he lowered himself to his knees. "Father, in a few minutes I fully intend to go into this town and seize control in your name. The things that have been done are wrong, and I will deal with those responsible. Help me, God, do those things which must be done." He felt something touch his forehead and jumped back a bit.

"Don't move or you will die instantly!"

He looked up to see the guard he'd noticed a few minutes before now standing over him. The man's sword was drawn and hovered a few inches from Mashua's face.

"I don't know why Commander Estigan called off the search and warned us to be careful, but you'll not be getting away from me."

Mashua looked into the man's face and saw beads of sweat on his brow. The man had assumed Mashua was Idiptu's partner who had escaped the previous afternoon. Mashua knew nothing of where his two friends had gone, but it was obvious to him this man was frightened. Not knowing the guard's intentions, he knew if he could get the sword away from him it would be easy to overpower him. The guard, knowing his orders, had no intention of hurting Mashua but hoped to take him as a prisoner until he could be sure of his identity. However, Mashua had no intention of being captured. The guard lowered his sword to his side, and Mashua saw his opportunity to jump him. Just as he poised himself to pounce upon the unprepared guard, he heard a little voice in his head tell him to go with the man peacefully.

Mashua stood up. He was easily a head taller and much broader than the guard. This did no good for the other man's composure.

"Fine," said Mashua, "I could easily break you in half." The man, trembling, raised his sword a bit. "However, I will allow you the dignity of capturing me. Does that make you feel better?"

The guard nodded and pointed his sword down the street in the direction of Commander Estigan's home.

When they arrived at the Commander's home, Idiptu and the Commander were sitting at the table eating breakfast. Idiptu still refused to answer any of Commander Estigan's questions except in vague and distracting ways. The Commander desperately wanted to know everything in detail, but as he had learned nothing at all, he had made up an agenda for Idiptu. His assumption was that Idiptu worked directly for Coracus. For some reason, the Emperor had not only sent these spies to Afeena but had also sent some sort of an invading force that had already overtaken the island and had hidden themselves everywhere. This force had arrived before Idiptu and his friend. The Commander had been assured that it would be useless to resist and that, unless he came clean of all his evil deeds, all of which Coracus (referred to by Idiptu as his majesty) already was aware of, he would soon be destroyed. However, a lot of Estigan's assumptions did not make any sense, so he continued to ply Idiptu with kind words and drink.

"Very soon," Idiptu smiled and said, "the rest of my team will arrive, and we will discuss your mismanagement during your time here. If I were in your shoes, I would begin to determine how I might make corrections."

Commander Estigan was at a loss for the presence of these people. The last time he had reported to the island commander in Artuna, nothing had been said about any error he had committed. However, he knew on Akadon and Leetra there would need to be no cause for dismissal or even death. If one fell into disfavor with the hierarchy, he could only wait for the inevitable punishment. Afeena had not been a bad assignment, as one was not under Coracus' nose and had more latitude. The old man, as people called Coracus behind his back, had grown fearful, for both good reasons and foolish assumptions, that he was in imminent peril. There had been attempts on his life. He had a very unusual way of running his administration. A person might work for years in gaining favor and receiving promotions through the ranks. Then, for no reason at all, find himself cast into prison or executed. Often, his replacement would be an untrained underling or even a slave or prisoner. The current deputy commander of Leetra had spent many years in prison, until one day, he was released and immediately promoted to his current position. The terror was, therefore, accepted among the bureaucracy on the other two islands to keep everyone in line. Now, it seemed, Coracus wanted to strengthen his hand on Afeena.

The other means of maintaining control was the almost total lack of communication or transportation between islands or even between towns. All of the main sailing vessels were maintained at the port in Akadon. There were no ships assigned permanently to Leetra or Afeena. No ship sailed without Coracus' personal approval.

The only method of travel in Estigan's territory was by foot. The island commander had a few horses. Even if Estigan was required to contact Commander Borda, the Island Commander, he would have to send one of his men on foot to reach him. It was a five-mile trek to the south side of the island to send a message. Therefore, Estigan normally waited until someone came to see him.

Due to his constant fear of reprisal for any of his shortcomings, he was not surprised that a spy had arrived at his door. Because of his out-of-the-way location, he had grown lax. He had been instructed to exercise his best judgment in exacting some type of punishment on a certain family only the day before and had not yet carried it out. This had become fairly routine. If someone had betrayed him, it would be his word against theirs.

"If I knew the exact nature of your visit, I could more easily accommodate your requests," he calmly explained.

"But, Commander Estigan, I have made no requests. I have merely suggested that you consider your actions here and warned you that I am not alone."

There was a rap at the door.

"Come in!" Commander Estigan called. "The door is open."

The door opened, and Idiptu was taken by surprise to see Mashua escorted by a guard whose sword was drawn.

Chapter 5

"I thought you were hurt yesterday when I saw you."

Ahohiel was surprised again by his little friend. Lora had visited him several times since they had met yesterday, but this time she had caught him praying again. During her several visits, she had continuously brought him various things to eat and kept his water jar full.

"Have you kept our secret?"

She nodded. "My mommy has been busy helping my daddy with company."

"Who is your company?"

She had come in and sat beside him. "I don't know. Some man from one of the other islands. I think Daddy's scared of him. Sometimes they are very mean."

"What mean things have they done to you?" he asked tenderly. He had grown to care strongly for this little girl and feared any harm coming to her if he were discovered.

"They have my big sister and won't let me even see her." Until now she had always spoken quite innocently. Now, however, tears began to fill her eyes and her lips quivered uncontrollably.

He couldn't help himself. He drew her to him and hugged her gently as she cried. "Oh, Lora," he said, "I am so sorry. I didn't know."

She stopped crying and looked into his eyes. "That's why I like you and made you my friend. I miss my sister. Her name is Regina."

"I understand, honey. Let's pray." She looked at him doubtfully. "You watch what I do. Dear God, I have a request. Please, if you will answer it, bring Lora and her sister back together real soon. I feel in my heart you will do this. Thank you, Lord."

She glanced around. "What is God? Is he around here?"

"Yes, Lora. He is here in my heart. Would you like him to be in your heart?" She quickly nodded. "Then you say what I say, but you have to really mean it."

"I would do anything you ask me to."

"Repeat after me. Dear God." He spoke slowly as she repeated. "I am sorry for all the bad things I have done. I want you to help me be a better little girl. I want you in my heart. Please come into me now. Thank you, God."

He gently cupped her face in his hands and asked her if she knew what had happened. She nodded her head and stood up. "I have to go now, or I'll be in trouble." She ran out of the shed and back to the house. He wondered if he had made any difference in her.

Chapter 6

The moment Mashua had walked into the room, he began to take control. He first walked directly to Idiptu and asked him in their secret tongue if he was fine. Then, they briefly discussed what could have happened to Ahohiel.

Commander Estigan politely tried to interrupt, but as he was ignored, he decided to sit quietly. He assumed Mashua was also working for Coracus, and it would not be wise to meddle. Then Mashua turned on him.

"The things you have done here are inexcusable." Estigan stood up and tried to explain. "Sit down and be quiet!" The Commander crumbled back into his seat. "I realize you are only a petty village commander, but you have still committed crimes. Are you prepared to be totally honest with me, or would you like to wait on a higher authority?"

Estigan nodded his head. "I'll do whatever it takes to please you. Tell me what I have to do."

"I am not the least interested in being pleased!" Mashua snapped. "You are about to face the judgment of God!"

Estigan was dumbstruck. He stared back and forth at Mashua and Idiptu for a moment. "God? What are you talking about? Are you saying you do not work for Emperor Coracus?"

"I have never seen this imbecile, but I would be pleased to straighten him out as well."

Mashua was standing next to Idiptu, both of whom were watching the Commander intently. He never saw the broadside of the sword before it struck his skull. He sunk, unconscious, to the floor. Idiptu was held at sword point while both of them were bound securely.

"Quickly dispatch a message to Commander Borda," Estigan ordered. "Tell him we have captured these two revolutionaries and, though I believe they are working alone, we will immediately begin a search. However, I will need his help. Now run." Estigan assumed, as had the guard, that Mashua was the man who had escaped the day before. The guard left quickly and Estigan ensured his two prisoners were bound and gagged securely. Then, he went to the front door and rang the alarm to call the rest of his men.

As soon as Ahohiel heard the bell ringing, he fled into the woods.

After Commander Estigan had briefed his men on how to conduct their search and his two prisoners had been removed, he sat quietly smoking a cigar in his den. His daughter meekly poked her head into the doorway.

"Lora, my sweetheart. Come to Daddy." She smiled and calmly approached her father. "I am sorry that your mother and I have been too busy for you. So, what have you been up to?"

"I made a friend and we talked and talked."

Supposing it to be her childish imagination, he paid scant attention. "So, have you been a good girl?"

"Uh huh. I have God in my heart now to help me be a good girl."

"You have what?" he asked suspiciously.

She placed both her hands nervously over her mouth when she remembered her promise to Ahohiel.

"Lora, tell me what you have been up to."

"I can't, Daddy. I made a promise."

"Lora. Tell me what has happened. You want to be a good girl. You have to tell your father."

"But it will ruin his surprise."

He glared at her, and she started to cry.

Picking her up, he stroked her hair and held her. "Please tell me, darling. Tell me about your friend. I'll try not to ruin his surprise."

"He prayed that God would come in my heart and He did."

"Did you do anything else?"

"I gave him some stuff to eat." Estigan nodded. "Then we prayed the best prayer ever."

"You say you prayed, but our family has never prayed."

"I know, but he showed me how. I can show you."

"Not now," he said, shaking his head, "but, what was your best prayer?"

"Regina will come home very soon!"

He looked into her eyes and could see her total trust and belief that this would happen.

"Umm. Lora, Regina can't come home for a long time."

"But he said…"

"I know. I know. Why don't you show me where he is and I'll ask him."

Reluctantly, she climbed down and led him out the back door to the tool shed. Ahohiel was gone, but the bowls she had been carrying the food and water in were still there.

"I don't know where he is, Daddy. He didn't say good-bye."

They walked back into the house, and he explained to his wife what had taken place. She looked Lora over to ensure she hadn't been harmed by this stranger as Estigan went back to his den. Lora ran past him on the way into her room.

"What's the hurry?" he called.

She stuck her head out of the bedroom and said, "I want to clean my room so my sister will have a place to sleep." She disappeared back into her room.

"Lora!" As she didn't respond, he returned to his den. A few minutes later he heard a carriage rumble to a stop in front of his house.

Hurrying to the door and opening it, he was stunned to see a pretty red-haired teenage girl climbing down. He dropped his cigar on the walk.

"Father!" Regina ran to him and hugged and kissed him profusely. "Oh, Father, I am so glad to see you." There were tears in her eyes. When her mother and sister arrived, she was overcome with emotion and could hardly speak.

After making the rounds between the three of them several times, she finally stood before her father and stared into his confused face. "You haven't even said hello, silly."

"I...I am speechless. I don't understand." He glanced at his guard who had returned with the driver. The guard merely shrugged his shoulders.

"When I reached Artuna to tell him of our trouble here, she was just arriving at Commander Borda's house," the guard said. "We nearly met at the doorway, sir. I reported to him of our two prisoners, and he requested I return the two prisoners to him to be immediately sent to Leetra for questioning. He asked me to escort your lovely daughter here. If there's nothing else, sir, I'll be leaving to get the prisoners now and we'll take the coach back. I'll take care of this alone because I know," he glanced at Regina, "you will be very busy."

"Yes, of course." The guard quickly departed, and Estigan looked back at Regina. "But how?"

She shook her head. "I don't know, Father." She waved her hands about. "A week ago, I was on Akadon working and my overseer called me and said I had been granted permission to take the first boat out to Afeena and go home. I am not stupid. I didn't ask very many questions. Unfortunately, there are not many boats leaving from Getz, so it took some time."

Lora took Regina's hand. "Come inside. I knew you were coming, so I fixed your bed."

Still stunned, Estigan and his wife stared at each other for several moments before going inside.

Chapter 7

Anam sat in a circle with the women. "It's been three hours since he left. It almost seems as if it is back to just us, like old times. We've all been in deep thought and prayer since he left. Any advice?" He glanced back and forth at the three of them

"Let's persevere just a bit longer," said Crazon. "Let's truly ask the Lord what we should do next."

They all clasped hands and bowed their heads in silence. Almost immediately, Zoana spoke up. "I just had the clearest picture in my mind. They are in trouble. I am sure of it."

"What did you see, sister?" Crazon asked.

"I saw Mashua and several other men being forced into a sailing ship."

"Were Ahohiel and Idiptu there?" she asked.

Zoana's expression seemed very far away as she attempted to see in her spirit what was happening. "I don't know," she said quietly. "Mashua had been bleeding from his forehead and no one had cared for the wound. He was stumbling along like he was still dazed. I...I can't seem to identify anyone else with him. Except for Mashua, everything else is all sort of blurry, but there were armed guards and several prisoners." She closed her eyes and concentrated on the vision. A few moments later, she looked blankly at Anam. "There is a prison on Leetra. They are taking them to Leetra."

Anam nodded. "I feel this is a clear vision from God. I also feel we should depart for Leetra as rapidly as we are able," He stood up and glanced around their empty campsite. "It won't take long to break camp." He reached down and strapped his knife belt around his waist. All his other weapons were gone, "There," he smiled, "I guess I'm ready. Let's go after the boat."

It had been easy for them to carry the boat quite a way from the beach with everyone helping before. Now, with just the four of them, they laboriously dragged the boat back to the water. Soon, they were once again afloat. Traveling was vastly more difficult now. The wind was not favorable at all. However, when conditions were unfavorable before, Mashua had nearly always been able to pick up a breeze and get them going in the right direction. They were at a great disadvantage without his ability and Idiptu's navigational skills. Now, they were forced to paddle. It was slow, hot, hard work. Though they were certain they were headed in the general direction of Akadon and Leetra, that evening as it grew dark, depression began to set in as there was still no land in sight. They feared drifting and getting lost at sea during the night, but as the anchor did not reach the bottom, they didn't know how to stabilize the boat. Physically, they were exhausted from rowing all day in the heat.

"Let's pray," Anam encouraged. They gathered together and each called upon God for strength and understanding. They commended themselves to God and all easily drifted off to sleep.

Early in the morning, they were awakened by the gentle pelting of rain. The sky, in the direction they traveled from, was dark and sinister. Actually, they had no idea where they were or which way to go. Lightning occasionally lit up the darkened eastern sky.

Anam nearly laughed. "I can't believe our run of luck. I realize there's not been any rain for two weeks, but why do we need this storm now? God! We need something nice to happen. Can you give us a hand?"

The water was beginning to get choppy. They all realized at once they had a favorable wind and cautiously raised the sail partway. The boat responded by nearly flying across the water. They all let out a cheerful acclamation as they sped along, hopefully, in the right direction. Soon they were rewarded when they saw land. However, the storm continued to grow in intensity as it overshadowed them. Approaching the shoreline, they began to encounter dangerous rocks. They did not want to lower the sail now for fear they would be stranded in the rocky area when the full force of the storm hit. However, as they sped along, they grazed across many of the rocks.

Suddenly, as the water pulled away from one fairly flat rock, the boat fell upon it with a loud thud and cracked the bottom of the hull. When the wave came crashing back, the craft was nearly capsized as it fell over the edge of the rock.

"We've got to get off this thing!" Paluqua yelled to Anam as she held on tight. "It's not helping us anymore."

"We are close to shore," he agreed. "I think we can make it if we leave the boat."

They glanced at the other two women and he waved at them, indicating they should follow. He dove in. The water was not deep and, most of the time, his feet were able to touch the bottom. He motioned toward shore and started to struggle in that direction. Crazon and Paluqua quickly followed him. Zoana, now left alone in the boat, was prepared to dive but suddenly glancing about at the storm and menacing waves, she froze up. Though only hesitating a few seconds, that was nearly fatal. Just as she regained her confidence, the front end of the boat landed on another large rock. As the water pulled away, the boat flipped over backwards. When she saw the boat coming down upon her, she attempted to protect herself. The full force of the boat landed on her shoulder and neck as she tried to pull away.

Unconscious now, she slipped to the bottom of the shallow water. The other three had seen everything and forced their way back to the capsized boat.

It was a simple task for Anam to find her and help her to restore breathing, but it was cumbersome for him to head back toward shore fighting the waves and carrying her. Crazon and Paluqua helped as much as they could, and eventually, they made it to the narrow beach.

Zoana was breathing now, though still dazed and unable to move about. While the two women helped her and prayed over her, Anam looked around at their landing site. Despite the weather, he could see for a great distance in both directions until the curve of the beach disappeared. The beach was but a strip of land shielded from the inland by a wall of stone as far as he could see. However, at least for now, they were safe.

Chapter 8

Mashua snapped awake. For a moment he could not remember where he was. He vaguely remembered slopping around in the hold of a ship with several other people. He had no idea how he had gotten there. He had no idea where he was now, except that he was enveloped in total darkness. The pain in his head was still throbbing. However, what was causing the stabbing pains in his back he knew not. When he attempted to touch his back, he realized both wrists were manacled to the wall. He could not remember any chains in the ship, but he was certain he was on land now. Finally, reaching the nape of his neck with the back of his hand, he was rewarded with a surge of pain. Obviously, he had been whipped or beaten while unconscious. He coughed to clear his throat.

"Mashua," he heard Idiptu out of the darkness. "Are you awake?"

"I think so," he mumbled. "I wish I were sleeping and having a nightmare. Where are we?" he spoke up.

"Quietly, friend. They don't take kindly to any sort of noise. We are, I think, on Leetra in an underground dungeon or some kind of jail."

"Were we on a boat with some other people?"

"Yes, there were eight of us; all men or boys. Apparently, the rest were just being rounded up from their families so their lives could be made miserable. We are considered to be a little more dangerous than that. I don't think the rest of our people are here."

"What hit me?"

"Well, when the spirit welled up in you in front of that commander, the guard whacked you over the head with his sword. They thumped on you a lot the last couple of days. You were out most of the time and they were hot-tempered."

"So, what's next?"

"I don't know. We've been in here a while. I don't know how long. They came in once and gave me a drink. You were out, so they ignored you. No one has said anything about what's going on."

"Let's pray," Mashua said. "I'll start. Oh, Father," he said quietly. "Sometimes we don't know why we get into the situations we do. A lot of it probably is caused because we're not too bright. If my rashness was out of your will, I am sincerely sorry." He started to pray in their secret tongue to which they'd grown accustomed. "All I know is that you are God and I am yours. I thank you for whatever situation I am in because I realize you are always in charge."

Idiptu spoke up. "Yes, Almighty God, you are in charge."

Without realizing it, they began to speak up and pray at once, not because they desired to compete with each other, but because they began to forget where they were. As their praise and words to God began to reach a crescendo, a voice from outside the cell yelled in to be silent. They only barely noticed the distraction but began to pray in the Denarite tongue again.

Something collided with the dark prison door. "I said to shut up." They both stopped and glanced in the direction of the noise before continuing again more quietly. However, not for long, as the volume of their voices continued to rise. A few minutes later, the cell door opened and two guards, each bearing a torch, entered. The one in front was fairly heavy and the elder of the two. Both men approached the Denarites timidly. The elder one spoke.

"Look," he said gruffly, "what do I have to do to get you two quiet?" Idiptu had stopped and was looking at the two men. However, Mashua had not missed a word. The two guards glared at him. "Hey!" he yelled. Mashua stopped. "What do you think you're doing?"

"We're praising our creator," said Mashua. "We thank him for everything as he is in charge of everything."

The older guard laughed. "You can thank him for being chained in this rathole?"

"I would rather spend a thousand years chained in this dungeon than to have my immortal soul burn in Hell because I forgot my God."

The two guards were silent for a moment. The elder one seemed exasperated. "Look, I wouldn't mind so much except the other prisoners can hear you."

"Then there are other prisoners?" asked Idiptu.

"Of course."

"Yes. Praise God!" said Mashua as he started again. "Your awesomeness is so overpowering my Lord. Your love is so great and so gentle. Your understanding can reach us in any place. You are the Mighty God! You always have the victory!"

The elder guard put his hand over his face and yelled, "If there is a God, help me deal with this!"

Idiptu spoke up again. "You know we have been in here a long time and he has had nothing to drink. Neither of us have eaten."

"Sholl," he addressed the younger man, "go fetch some water for these two and see if there is any bread left out front."

"Yes, sir!" The man ran off.

"My name is Lanao. I am in charge of the prison. I can't run a prison with all this noise. I realize you don't want to be here."

Mashua stopped him and spoke. "We never said we didn't want to be here. We thanked God for placing us here."

"Yes, I suppose you did. But, why?"

"Well, in the first place, why not? I mean if we didn't give him the credit, we'd have to give it to Satan. We don't want to do that. In the second place, we feel we are here as part of a divine plan. Do you believe in God?"

He sat on the dusty floor and reflected for a moment. "I think so. I'm not sure. The Emperor Coracus says he was placed in his office by God."

"And, in that, he is correct," said Idiptu. "However, he has misused his office. We are all where we are because God has placed us there. If we don't use our wisdom in acting godly wherever our office is, whether as an emperor or anyone else, God will have us in his hand on Judgment Day." He held out his hand. "Now he extends the hand of love and kindness like a caring father. On that day, he will dispense judgment and reward for what we have done."

Lanao glanced nervously over his shoulder. "What could be keeping that boy? Sholl!" he called out. He looked back at Idiptu. "What were we talking about?"

"Judgment Day," said Mashua. "Fully accepting the Almighty God as the Lord over our lives and then following his will for us."

"Oh. I see," he said. He sat in silence for quite a while. Finally, he spoke up, "I am really confused. I know I've done wrong. I certainly haven't thought much about God." He grew quiet again. "Tell me what to do."

"Repeat after me," said Idiptu. "You must be very sincere." He prayed slowly as Lanao repeated his words. "Dear Father, I know I have committed terrible sins against both you and many people. I cannot fix all the wrong I've done, so I ask you to work in me and forgive me anyway, though I don't deserve it. I want to be your son and for you to be my father. I want to be part of the family of God. I want to work for you and someday join you in heaven. Thank you, God."

When Idiptu looked back at Lanao, he was only slightly surprised to see tears in the man's eyes glistening in the torch light.

"I feel at the same time unworthy and, also, so good. I don't understand, but I feel real good." He smiled. "If God is my Father, and yours, that makes us brothers, right?"

Idiptu nodded. He held up his hands with the chains clanking. "Is this what you do to your brothers."

Lanao couldn't speak for a moment. "I'm not sure what I should do." He put his hand on Mashua's shoulder to support himself as he stood up. Mashua clenched his teeth and moaned in great pain. Holding his torch over Mashua, he could see his back. "Those damn fools! They tore your back up bad, and you weren't even conscious to know it. Just a minute. Sholl!" he called out again as he turned and stumbled into his assistant. "Oh, there you are. Where were you?"

Sholl stood holding a jug of water and a tray of dry bread. "I was standing right here most of the time, but I didn't want to interrupt. Sir, is everything all right?"

Lanao surprised Sholl by patting him on the shoulder. "Sholl, everything is absolutely wonderful. Everything is grand."

Chapter 9

"Your excellency, your transportation awaits its departure to Leetra. I trust you are prepared."

"Uh, yes. I suppose."

Coracus had been letting his mind wander among a multitude of affairs, chief among them was this disturbing report of two men appearing on Afeena and convincing Commander Estigan they worked for himself. No one knew where they came from. Then, this talk of God. That also disturbed him.

He looked at his chamberlain, Daga, standing over him. A heavy wrap was draped over Daga's arm. His face glistened with moisture. He realized the man had been out in the rain. His boots were soaked through, though most of the rest of his clothes were dry as he had removed his overcoat. He was dressed for summer, with shorts and a light shirt, except for his heavy boots. Though Daga was as old as Coracus, he kept his body in shape with constant workouts. His face, however, was drawn and withered. Coracus had never noticed before how old Daga looked in the face. He suppressed a smile as he realized Daga looked like a thirty-year-old man with an eighty-year-old head. His head even seemed small for his body.

He looked him in the eye. Something seemed to be bothering him. "Is it still raining outside, then?"

"Yes, sir. It's coming down in huge buckets."

"Must I travel in the rain?"

"You do not have to travel at all, your majesty. However, you ordered me to make haste and let nothing hold up your travel as soon as you received the message from Leetra about these two."

"So, I did. So, I did. There was a time I liked the challenge of forcing a craft against the weather. Daga, is there something the matter?"

Coracus caught him off guard, and he could not answer immediately. Daga gazed down at the old man. He could see he no longer had the suppleness of youth. There had been a time when his mere presence was threatening and dynamic. They had grown up through the ranks together. He had always been one step behind Coracus and proud of it.

As young boys they had volunteered to be palace guards. Their overpowering personalities ensured their positions. Coracus had moved up as company commander, personal bodyguard to the old president and general of the army. For a time, Daga's position had occasionally overshadowed his until he had been caught in a conspiracy and the old president had him imprisoned. Eventually, Coracus had successfully petitioned for his release and return to his position as a palace guard. Then, about twenty years ago, they had hatched a plot, and in one night, assassinated the president, reorganized the army and government, and finally taken over Leetra and Akadon. They had foolishly allowed a multitude to flee to Afeena in their haste to take over. Thereafter had followed years of enmity between the two domains. Then, two years before, Daga had with Coracus' nod, moved in force on Afeena and conquered them. They were now totally subdued. However, this had all been Daga's battle.

"I'm sorry, sir" he snapped out of his reverie. "I am concerned about your trip in this awful weather. It rained all day yesterday. I was certain today it would pass."

"And that's all that's bothering you?"

Daga was careful not to change his expression. Coracus had grown suspicious of everyone, even his best friend. Daga had seen and been part of the systemic cleansing of death of those closest to the palace. However, he had never been suspected by Coracus of any foul play against himself. It was difficult to appear nonchalant and not allow certain distractions from entering his mind.

"I am concerned for your well-being, Excellency."

Coracus forced a smile. "Always thinking of me. How would I have made it all these years without your great self-sacrificing attitude? You shall be remembered in history as one of the most honorable men ever."

"You are too kind, sir. I follow you because of your power and charisma. I always have. I've always felt honored by being one step behind you."

Coracus moved forward in his seat as he prepared to get up. "One step behind me? Yes, but a step ahead as well." Daga looked questionably at his leader. "You have so often cleared the way for me. Then, you give me the honor. You have done well." He took Daga's hand to help himself stand. Once up, he felt of his chamberlain's palm. "Your hands are so sweaty, my friend."

Daga looked at the palms of his hands and wiped them on his shirt. "They are not sweaty, sir. I have been out in the rain preparing the skiff."

"Oh yes, so you were. Will you be going with me?"

"Not this time. There are six soldiers and the crew as well as both of your interrogators."

Coracus nodded as Daga assisted him with his coat. "I would prefer you came. This could be most interesting."

"I have made no plans to travel, sir. To change things now, we would simply have to cancel and make the trip later.

Ask yourself, Excellency, do you prefer my company or are you urgent to discover what these two troublemakers are all about? Besides, someone needs to attend to duties here. Who would you have me appoint? Is there anyone you can trust more than myself?"

Coracus waved his hands in the air. "Fine, stay if you must! I'll take care of this myself!" he snapped.

"I did not mean to offend, sir." Daga lowered his face.

Coracus stormed off toward the docks by himself, not waiting for the guards. When they appeared in the doorway to escort Coracus, Daga simply waved in the direction of the opposite doorway, indicating he'd already left. They proceeded to hurriedly march toward the skiff. Daga pulled their leader aside.

"You have done as instructed, Veaga?"

"Yes, sir!" replied the captain. "Four of the planks at the bottom of the boat have been all but removed. A hard whack will knock them loose. The boat will sink almost at once. And the other boat?"

"The rescue vessel will proceed just out of sight of your vessel. They will observe your actions with the scope. As soon as you leave the skiff, they will snatch you up from the water. Your only responsibilities will be to sabotage the skiff, leave it before anyone is aware, and remain afloat until the rescue vessel arrives. If you do not fail me," Daga jabbed his finger nearly in the man's face, then lowered it and smiled, "you will be promoted to the rank of general when we reorganize the army tomorrow."

Veaga boldly crossed his arms in front of himself and stated, "Have no fear of that, Emperor. I shall not fail you."

Daga brought both his hands thoughtfully to his lips. "Emperor? Hmm, I like that title, General." They nearly shook hands but thought better of it in case there were spies. "Farewell. I hope you have a simply lovely trip."

The captain saluted him and quickly followed his men to the boat dock.

Daga strolled around the palace for a few minutes, speaking with the servants and guards in an unnaturally friendly way. There weren't many people around, as it was quite early. He nearly terrified one young girl by carrying a bucket of water for her. Then, he returned to Coracus' sleeping quarters, informed the guard he wanted to sit there and meditate for a bit, and entered the room. After bolting the door, he glanced around cautiously. Though he had been there a countless number of times, now he felt nervous. Looking at the veranda window to ensure no one was spying on him, he decided not to open the outside door. It was too nasty out. Finally, feeling his confidence return, he walked over to the four-poster bed and kicked off his heavy boots. He lay down on the bed coverings in his clothes to take a nap.

Their departure from Akadon had been quite mild. For a time, the rain had slackened to occasional sprinklings. However, though it was now late in the morning, the sky was still dark. When they had reached the midpoint between the islands, the weather worsened considerably. The crew was able to stay on course only with great difficulty. Daga's hireling saw his chance to do his job. Without Daga's knowledge, Veaga had actually paid off one of the crewmen to do the work below before they left. A casual inspection would show nothing amiss and that part of the plan had gone well.

Veaga saw the crewman glance in his direction and he gave him a nod. The man left to finish his dirty work. Veaga would wait for about a minute and they would rendezvous above. Casting his vision briefly at Coracus and each of the other guards, he sensed no one suspected anything. Most of them were contending with the nausea brought about by the vengeful waves.

Veaga leaned over to the guard closest to him and excused himself to go above and retch. The other man wearily nodded at him and paid no more attention. Veaga quietly slipped away. Above, the crew was busy trying to maintain the sails in the weather and going about their usual cursing. He met his crewman in their appointed place.

"You have followed orders?"

"Yes, sir! The lower hold is quickly filling with water now. In calm weather they could, perhaps, maintain stability and reach shore, but not in this foul weather."

"Excellent."

"You told me that Daga has promised us a rescue vessel. If he fails us, we shall also die." The man looked off into the storm from where they had traveled. "I see no one."

"You need to look more closely." As the crewman leaned over the edge of the boat, Veaga drew his blade, slit the man's throat and cast him into the sea. "There, my friend, you are rewarded for your treachery."

Quickly, Veaga moved toward the aft end of the boat and reached over to find a rope he had tied there earlier. Dragging the rope aboard, he was shocked to see nothing on the end. He heard laughter and looked around.

Coracus stood only a few paces from him, wearing a life vest. "Are you missing this, you stupid fool? You see, you were also duped. Daga never made arrangements for a rescue. His plan was that I and all aboard would be sadly lost at sea. No chance of retribution. However, there shall be a rescue, for I made the arrangements myself. Very soon, you will be able to once again enjoy the company of your treacherous friend."

Coracus dove overboard and Veaga ran to where he had stood. He saw a small craft approaching and drawing nearer to them. He could no longer see Coracus through the mist until the crew on the other vessel fished him from the sea. For a moment, he was stunned at the turn of events, until he ran off to find the captain and alert him of the danger.

"It was very wise telling us to lay over out of sight, your Excellency, until such time as you departed."

Coracus had replaced his cold and soggy regal clothing with dry plain wear and was relaxing in the captain's chair. "I am no fool. I did not attain this position by following others stupidly. Now, everyone on Akadon knows you returned to Leetra several hours ago. All the other vessels are accounted for. When the other ship never arrives, Daga will surely believe all were lost, myself especially."

"I must attend to other matters, sire. We will be arriving on Leetra in a few minutes. Two of our guards will escort you to the prison. Any observers will be certain you are a prisoner. I wish you the very best."

Coracus, still shivering from his dowsing, lay back in the chair, pulled the blanket around his chin and closed his eyes.

"We are escorting this prisoner under Coracus' direct orders," one of his escorts informed Lanao. "He must be harbored with the other two radicals."

"But, like I explained," said the prison magistrate, "he cannot be secured there as it is fully occupied. He would have to roam free."

"Then, he'll roam free! Our directions are to secure him with the other two prisoners and ask no questions. You are to ask no questions, either. Simply lock him up."

"But for the record?"

The guard shook his head. "Just lock him up with no record. I am certain that, later on, all the mystery will be made clear to you."

Therefore, figuring this new prisoner to be some sort of spy, Lanao agreed and escorted the two guards and new prisoner back to where Mashua and Idiptu were still in chains. Earlier, he had released them both, fed them, and tended to Mashua's wounds. When he heard there were guards at the outer door, he had instructed Sholl to re-secure them until he could verify who was coming in. He was not pleased that this new prisoner would be with his friends as he had intended to let them roam freely after this nuisance had been attended to. Now his mind raced as to who this man could be. He had assumed when the information on the new prisoners had been sent to Akadon, someone would come and investigate. This, however, was unusual. It crossed his mind that this man could even be an assassin. He intended to defend his new friends with his own life, if need be. Near the entrance to the cell, he stopped.

"As a regular precaution, this prisoner should be searched and sacrifice most of his garb."

The guard shook his head. "He is to be locked up with the other two. No questions!" he snapped.

He unlocked the door, and the unidentified prisoner entered the murky cell. The prisoner and guard exchanged a few whispers as Lanao walked away, muttering under his breath. Glancing over his shoulder, he caught them unaware as the guard saluted the other man. There were few who would qualify for such a salute.

Lanao went back to his room and pondered this. He could not fathom that Coracus himself would come into his prison as a criminal and subject himself to imprisonment and danger. The Emperor had used spies in the past, and sometimes prisoners were even admitted to spy on himself. But he could not understand the salute to someone of low estate. He also feared this agent could be an assassin. He had lost other prisoners that way. They would die in an unusual way before their embarrassing testimonies could be made public. Then, the assassin would normally be executed for murder.

However, he was not concerned for an assassin's damaging effects on his own reputation, but he had truly befriended Idiptu and Mashua. He couldn't explain it. He wanted to learn more from them. His fear of reprisal should he break the guard's word bothered him, but his fear of losing his two friends was greater.

When Coracus had entered the cell and the door had been closed, he was plunged into darkness. Under the light of the torch, he had seen a place to sit, so he had stumbled across the room in the dark and found it. He had also seen the two prisoners, only for a moment, watching the activity. He had desired to come here under complete anonymity. It had been a stupid blunder on behalf of the guard to salute him and, if it jeopardized his plan, the guard would suffer for it.

The three of them sat in the dark stillness for a couple of minutes. Finally, Mashua spoke up. "Well, my friend, what was your transgression to now be afforded room and board from the Emperor?"

While Mashua talked, Idiptu had begun praying. Coracus sat in silence. For the first time in his life, he felt speechless and could not understand why. Suddenly the cell door opened, and the keeper entered, carrying a bucket.

"If anyone wants water, there is plenty." He looked at Coracus, whose face was covered. "I do not know who you are, stranger. However, I am duty bound to protect my prisoners and shall do that exact thing. I was told you operated under orders from the Emperor." Coracus glanced at the prisoners and was enraged that his secret was revealed to them. Tomorrow, he thought, there would be a new prison magistrate. "Since I have been instructed to ask no questions," Lanao continued, "I will obey. However, if my prisoners are harmed, you shall deal personally with me. Is that understood?" Coracus did not immediately answer the question as he was considering what revenge he would bring down on Lanao. Lanao stepped forward and made as to grab hold of Coracus.

Coracus threw the cover off from his head. "You imbecile. Can you not follow simple orders?" Lanao froze in position. "You are in front of your Emperor. You had best be on your knees."

However, as much as Lanao desired to fall to his knees and beg forgiveness, he could not move. He could not even think straight.

Chapter 10

"But why did I hesitate? You know my nature. I usually just charge right in."

Zoana sat facing Anam across an evening campfire, which he had constructed under an overhanging rock. Paluqua and Crazon had left to seek food and better shelter and to make contact with the natives, if there were any. He had stayed with Zoana, as she had been groggy all afternoon and evening until now and could not be moved. Walking with her would have been difficult. Climbing would have been impossible. The main storm seemed to have passed, but a light rain continued to fall. She had, in the accident, pulled her neck and been struck in the forehead when the boat came down on her.

"I believe you have a fear of water from your ordeal last year in the mountains."

"But we've prayed about that."

Anam shrugged his shoulders. "I noticed on the way here that when everyone else had little fear of swimming in the ocean, you were very reluctant."

She grimaced as she tried to stretch the pain out of her neck. Anam moved around behind her, straddled her, and began a gentle massage of her neck and shoulders.

"Oh, thank you," she sighed. "That's wonderful. When will Paluqua and Crazon return?"

"We didn't say. I hoped they would return before night-fall." He paused, leaned over, glanced at the sky and returned to his work. "Who can tell when it's night? It's always dark. I suppose they'll return when they have discovered something worth discussing. Are you tired?"

"I'm not really tired, but my whole body feels tight with cramps."

"Then why don't you lie face down and I'll try to massage you to sleep."

She lay down on the sand and Anam gently, but firmly, massaged her from head to foot. As he finished, he sensed her whole body go limp and realized she had fallen asleep. He sat back, wishing he had a blanket to cover her from the drizzle that made its way into their little enclave. Sliding back to the wall, he found a position where he could comfortably sit up, and soon, he fell asleep as well.

A few minutes later, he was awakened by Crazon's and Paluqua's return, arriving from the opposite direction from which they had departed.

"Well, I hope you are enjoying our little retreat," Paluqua said sarcastically. She smiled at Anam as she moved over to where he was. "It doesn't get any more exciting than this. The whole island is only about five miles around, and the whole thing looks just like this." She waved her arms toward the beach.

"There was no place we could easily depart from the beach," chimed in Crazon. "It's pretty dull. Everywhere is beach and this wall. Of course, I'm sure the lovely weather doesn't help any. We couldn't see much. We did find these." Crazon had carried a large branch from some shrub back and now passed it to Anam. It was covered with tiny plums. "As we had nothing to carry the fruit in, we decided to bring a whole branch. There's actually a small orchard of these trees."

Anam tasted one. "These are delicious," he said.

"How's our sleepy one?" Crazon asked as Zoana sat up and stretched.

"Much better. Oh, these look good," she said as she noticed the plums.

As Anam and Zoana ate, Paluqua explained their trip. "We could easily circle this island in less than two hours, at a slow walk. This ridge and the sandy beach are all we really saw. There are lots of those," she indicated the plums. "About a mile back up the beach is a fairly extensive orchard if we want more."

Crazon laughed. "We saw the campfire quite a way up the beach. We were excited that we had finally discovered other people. I just can't believe how small this island is."

"It's pretty clear we're not on Akadon," said Paluqua. "However, I remember from Idiptu's map that there was a little island north of Akadon. We must have turned aside last night and stumbled here by mistake."

"Well," said Anam, "let's just hope the tide doesn't come in just before sunup. Let's try to get some sleep and then penetrate this island in the morning."

"Agreed!" Paluqua and Crazon both said at once.

"You know," said Paluqua. "This is really weird. I mean, we've landed on just about every island here. We've seen no one. But, one by one, our comrades have been swept away. I kept thinking how awful things are going. But I really believe God has his hand in all of this. Let's pray before we go to sleep."

They pulled together and prayed over their situation. Then, they took turns praying for the ones who had been separated from them. It seemed they were done, but Paluqua waited.

"Lord," she finally said, "if also somehow Marcis has survived, you keep your hand upon him and guide him. I know his faith isn't as strong as the others, so please, he needs your help." She looked at Anam. "I think he's still alive," she stated firmly.

The following morning, the four Rasomites followed the path Crazon and Paluqua had gone the evening before. Zoana, except for the bruise on her forehead, seemed to be fine. The inclement weather, though it was still upon them, had slowed to an occasional sprinkle. However, the horizon was still dark, so they expected more rain. They considered dousing the campfire, but when Anam explained how difficult it had been to get it started the day before and that they fully expected to be back in a couple of hours, it was left to burn.

As had been explained by the women the evening before, the island was pretty desolate. On the south side of the island, they found a large cleft in the wall with a natural path leading up the hill. There had been several places they could have easily scaled the wall; however, this particular spot was too inviting to pass up.

A few minutes later they had followed the path to one of the highest points on the island overlooking the sea and, hopefully, also Akadon. Unfortunately, just as they reached the top, the sky let loose with another torrent of rain, and they had nowhere to hide.

"Is everyone enjoying their scenic view?" Anam asked. "Later, we can relax on the shore."

"But look." Zoana pointed off to the east. In the distance, beyond the dark and sinister covering they were currently under, was blue sky. "We should be high and dry in a little while. We just need to be patient."

"I suppose," said Anam, "we needed the rain to make things grow. But God could have skipped this place because there's hardly anything growing anyway."

They sat down in the rain and waited for the weather to change. Sure enough, a few minutes later, the rain suddenly stopped, and the temperature began to rise. The view of the great open sea was breathtaking, and they sat for a while basking in the sun as they dried out.

"Anam, what are we going to do?" Zoana asked. "We are stranded here and Mashua and the others are locked up. We've made contact with no one. If we never get rescued, who will ever know we are here?"

They heard a noise behind them, and all spun around to see a haggard, old man bearing a harpoon. He was so malnourished he appeared to be all skin and bones. His only clothing was a skirt of ragged cloth wrapped about his waist. The harpoon was poised to be thrown. He mumbled a few words in the Denarite dialect of the islands, but they didn't understand him. Anam pointed at his ears and shook his head trying to indicate that he didn't know what was said.

"We are not from around here," he said. "We only know a little of your language."

The old man shook his head. Then he pulled at his skin and squinted at each of the Rasomites as he probably couldn't understand their skin color. Finally, he blankly glanced around at where they had been sitting, turned and walked away.

"That, women, was what happened to the last person who was stranded here. See what you have to look forward to." Then, he called out. "Wait!" All four ran after the strange man.

When he saw he was pursued he started to run, but his emaciated condition made it easy for them to catch up with him.

"We mean you no harm," Paluqua said. "Who are you?"

They had him surrounded against a large rock and he was trembling with fear. He nervously glanced back and forth as though seeking a chance to escape.

"He's terrified of us, Anam" she said. "Let's back off."

The four retreated a few paces and stood facing the old man. Anam sat down, and the three women followed. When he realized he was no longer being threatened, he also sat down, and they began a staring contest.

"Who are you?" Paluqua asked again. He made no response and merely kept staring at her. "He simply doesn't understand."

Anam smiled as he remembered a Denarite word. He patted his chest. "Name," he said in the Denarite tongue. "Anam." He pointed at his wife. "Name, Paluqua."

The old man tried to repeat her name but couldn't quite do it.

"Name, Zoana." Zoana said calmly. She glanced at Crazon.

"Name, Crazon," she said slowly.

The old man tried to move his mouth, but very little came out.

Anam pointed his finger at him. "Name?" he asked.

"Name." He repeated the word several times and almost seemed to give up. Then, he looked Anam in the eye, patted his chest and said, "Name, J...J..." he stuttered. Anam nodded encouragingly. "John." Anam clapped his hands a couple of times and was very pleased, but the old man raised his palm to stop him. "Name, John Dunley."

Everyone became very silent.

Chapter 11

When Commander Estigan had rung the bell to call his troops in, Ahohiel fled into the surrounding forest. Unaware the search had been called off, as his pursuers had he and Mashua confused, Ahohiel had spent an awful night in the open. The rain never stopped falling for the next full day. He had at first attempted to find some sort of shelter, but afraid the search was still on and he'd be found, he'd finally opted for an extremely uncomfortable position in the roots of a fallen tree. It offered very little protection.

The following afternoon when the rain began to let up, he crawled from his hiding place and decided to chance returning to his friends. It took a while to get his bearings, but eventually he found the creek bed that led back to their camp. He was shocked to find no one where he had expected them to be and, finally, wandered for a time along the shoreline. After thinking about it for a while, he thought perhaps he had started too far downstream, so he retraced his path and eventually was certain they had left. His next decision was that the group had either been captured or gone into town searching for himself and Idiptu. Once he was sure he had found the campsite, he quickly moved to where the boat had been secreted. Then, he sank to his knees in great dismay when he saw the boat missing and a trail broken through the brush in the direction of the beach.

"Oh, my God, no!" he cried. "Then, I'm deserted." The effects of exposure to the inclement weather, lack of food and sleep, and his exertion from several miles of roving back and forth were all added to this latest burden, and it was beyond him to deal with it all. He began to uncontrollably shiver and suddenly felt sick to his stomach. In the midst of vomiting, he passed out.

He woke up a few minutes later and, despite his vile appearance, merely sat up and stared blankly toward the beach. He moved his hand to his face and realized he was burning up with fever.

"What can I do?" he asked himself quietly. "Where can I go?" He realized his voice had a whiney, hopeless sound to it. "They must have fled. Why else would they leave?" He thought briefly about living in the relative comfort of little Lora's toolshed. "Don't let any harm come to that little servant of yours, Father."

He heard the birds chirping in the tree near him and watched them dance from branch to branch for a minute. "Your world is so beautiful, God. Thank you." Suddenly a stabbing pain seemed to ram into his forehead, and he nearly called out in anguish. His head still throbbing, he moved back toward the creek bed to get some fresh water and to wash up. Every step was painful, and he finally had to stop before reaching his goal.

Rolling into a ball with his arms wrapped about his head, he begged God to take away the pain. Finally, he got up and continued to stumble along. When he arrived at the water, he lay face down with his whole body in ankle-deep water. Then, he rolled over onto his back and took several deep breaths. Crawling back to dry land, he felt cooler and cleaner, but the pain in his head was still excruciating. Ahohiel leaned up against a tree and closed his eyes, wishing he could pass out again. Now he began to shiver as he had earlier, and dizziness came upon him. He resigned himself to sitting against the tree until the pain had passed. Then, suddenly, he was famished.

"God, what am I going to do?" he asked aloud. "My energy is spent. I hurt and I'm deserted and have nowhere to go. I guess this is when I run out of options and I have to rely on you. If I have done something foolish to put myself in this position and out of your will, I am sorry. Help me, Father. Please, help me." He was too tired and sickly to move or even to open his eyes, but as he sat there, he slowly began to feel better. His head stopped pounding and he sensed the fever begin to leave him. "Thank you, God." He was still too weary to get up.

Then he sensed someone watching him and opened his eyes. On the opposite bank sat the woman who had betrayed him and Idiptu. Nervously he glanced around, afraid of another betrayal.

"No. No, it's not like that." She quickly arose and splashed across the stream, stopping before him. Then she began to weep and touched his hand. "I am so sorry," she said. "I had a perfectly awful night. I could scarcely sleep. I know, I am sure, yours was worse. However, I have done a terrible thing. I didn't even think. When I left the house, I had sincerely planned to feed you and your friend. Then, an evil thought struck me, that if I turned you in, perhaps they would return my family. I miss them so much." She started to cry.

"It's fine," Ahohiel tried to comfort her.

"No, it was awful, and I was stupid. Coracus never keeps any promises to anyone on Afeena. He hates us. Commander Estigan could be a fine man. He gives us some space, but not the Emperor. However," she continued, "as soon as the guard had left with your friend, I felt so guilty. I felt absolutely terrible. I decided I must do something kind, but I didn't know what. Then, last night, I heard that both men had been taken prisoner to Leetra. However, when they described the other man, I was silent. I knew he could not be you as they described him as being a much larger man."

"Mashua," he interjected. "They have taken Mashua."

She shrugged her shoulders. "I knew you were still free and that no one was searching for you. I sought you in the rain last night until it was too dark, and I have been looking for you all day. I must beg of you; will you forgive me the terrible wrong I have done?"

"Yes," he nodded. "Yes, I forgive you. You have certainly redeemed yourself."

She kissed his hand and thanked him. "I have nothing to offer you. I couldn't possibly take you back into town as we would be discovered in a moment."

"What is your name?"

She was still holding his hand. "My name is Estella Edisni. And yours?"

"My name is Ahohiel. Your husband is a very fortunate man to have such a beautiful woman so devoted to him."

She slowly removed her hand from his. "I meant nothing by this gesture."

"I know that. Do you know I asked God to help me and he quickly sent you?"

"You believe in God?"

He nodded.

"I did not think anyone in the Isles believed in God anymore. He seems to have deserted us."

"He brought you to me, Estella. He has great power and He always has. God hasn't taken a vacation from here, but because of the hardness of peoples' hearts, evil has manifested itself. When people believe there is no hope, God has the greatest chance to truly reveal himself. We thought our people were totally without hope, but one day God arrived and changed everything."

Her face seemed to glow, and she said, "Where are you from?"

When he told her he was from Ifintim, she was shocked. He explained everything that had happened from the beginning and answered all of her questions. By the time he was finished with his story, it was beginning to grow dark.

"Would you feel brave enough to sneak into town in the dark?" she asked him. "If you would, I would let you stay in my house."

"Well," Ahohiel smiled, "I won't trust on my bravery. However, I will trust for God to protect me. I think it best if we don't show up together. You go in while it is still light. Once it's dark, I will come. I know your house."

She patted him on the arm. "Just come in the back door. This time it will be unlocked." She squeezed his hand and ran off toward town.

Ahohiel reflected on Estella. He knew from having been in her house she could only own a few scraps of clothing. He also knew she had been frantically looking for him in the rain all morning. He wondered how a woman of poverty as she was could be so lovely. Her darkish complexion was accentuated by her black hair. However, it was her eyes that were so mysterious. Whenever they had spoken this day, she would gaze into his eyes. A few times he had forgotten himself and lost his train of thought. He thought he could easily pick up her tiny body with one hand.

"My stupid friend," he said to himself aloud. "You need to cut it out. This little fawn that you are playing with in your mind is a married woman. She loves her family. She feels bad over her action of the other day and, hopefully, sees God in me." He prayed. "Dear God, keep my thought pure. Let me think, as Anam says, as though she were my sister. I will do all I can to lead her to you, Lord, and bring her precious family back together. I praise your name, Father. God, in a bit I shall be going back into town. Guide me and guard me, Father. Keep me in your path."

He dozed off for a few minutes and, when it was nearly dark, headed back to town. He thought it was unusually quiet, but he'd never roamed around at night in town before. It was easy to find Estella's house. There was no fence or obstruction in back since the yard ended where the trees began. It was an easy matter to get in as she had left the door unlocked and slightly ajar. He entered and sat on the floor for a moment. Looking about, he could see nothing had been changed in the barren room, except the window he had broken had been covered with several planks of lumber. He could hear Estella in the kitchen working so, cautiously and avoiding the windows, he went to her.

She was on her knees before the little stove with her back toward him, stirring a pot. Her hair descended almost to her waistline. The dress she wore was actually nothing more than a long shirt, almost floor length, and she wore leather sandals. He cleared his throat and she glanced over her shoulder with a smile on her face.

"I didn't hear you come in. You were so long I was afraid you would not come." Even from this position she was able to capture his eyes with hers.

Ahohiel swallowed the lump in his throat. "The Rasomites have taught me to travel silently." He hesitated. "Umm, Estella, I have a problem."

She stood up, facing him. "I am no longer afraid. I do not care what the repercussions are. I vow that I will help you the very best I can."

"Well." He looked away. "It's not that kind of problem. You see, you have intoxicated me."

She blushed and looked slowly at the floor. "I am sorry. I feel so ashamed. In my desire to convince you of my honesty, I guess I have overstepped the line. Will you forgive me again?"

They looked at each other and he laughed. "Of course, I forgive you. Will you forgive me?"

She nodded her head and pointed at the stove. "I have prepared a stew from the garden. I hope you like it."

"It smells wonderful and I've ate nothing since I left."

"Nearly three days?" she asked him surprised.

"Oh, no. I didn't tell you what happened when I left here. I spent a while in a little girl's tool shed."

"A tool shed?" She asked almost laughing. "Whose tool shed?"

"A little girl named Lora kept me the first night. She did a good job. She fed me and also accepted the Lord."

"Lora is Commander Estigan's daughter." She laughed out loud. "You were in the local Commander's backyard and they were searching for you in the forest. Let's sit. I'm sorry there are no chairs." They sat on the kitchen floor, and she scooped a generous bowl of stew for him. "And you say now she knows God?" Ahohiel nodded as he ate. "I want to know your God. Is that possible?"

"Of course," he said. He thought for a moment and sat down his bowl. "However, this is a very serious matter. Let me tell you what you need to do."

The next three weeks Ahohiel spent hiding out in Estella's home. During this time, she was very open to hear his testimony and how God had worked in his life. She had quickly accepted the Lord. It was difficult for him, but he managed to overcome his romantic interest in her. He forced himself to often call her sister to speed this process. Though it seemed odd to him, she received no visitors while he was there. She explained that no one had many visitors anymore because distrust was so great. However, one morning she seemed particularly distressed.

"What's wrong," he asked her. She shook her head. "Do you have secrets? Something is bothering you."

She sighed. "It's my neighbor. She often works in her garden when I do. This morning she stood watching me over the fence. I didn't think much of it until she asked me a question."

"And what was the question, sister?"

"She said, 'aren't you eating a terrible amount of food, Estella? By harvest time, you'll have nothing left.' I didn't think of it before. I thought we had been doing a good job keeping our secret."

"Perhaps it's nothing."

She smiled. "Perhaps it's nothing. But we cannot continue on like this forever. What are we going to do?"

"Well, we've prayed every day for God to intervene. This is when we need to be careful. More than before."

"More careful?" she asked. "Why now?"

"Because this is when we'll get tired of waiting and decide to do something on our own." She nodded. "We need to just be patient. I'm sure God will move quickly when he's ready."

"I know, but you have much more faith than I do. I have never really seen God work. Please, pray for me to be patient."

A short time later, as they were talking, a feeling came upon Ahohiel. "Estella, we are betrayed. We are in danger."

She threw her arms around him. "Oh, yes! I am sure of it, too. You must flee. If they find you here it will be worse for both of us." She kissed him. "Go into the woods and hide. I will come for you when I am sure it is safe."

They stared into each other's eyes for a moment, and he fled through the back door. However, he did not go far, rather staying close to the house to see what would happen. Sure enough, a few minutes later he saw two guards moving down the street and approach the house. One of the guards crept behind the house to guard the back door. Ahohiel smiled as he watched the man hide himself in the bushes only a few paces away. There was no activity after the other guard was admitted to the house. However, after several minutes in the house, the other guard opened the back door and called in his friend. A few minutes later, Ahohiel saw them proceeding back down the street with Estella bound between them.

Ahohiel felt like cursing and kicking something but restrained himself. Then, he thought this could even be part of God's plan. He knelt and prayed silently for guidance and heard God. "Yes, my son, this is part of my plan. Do not interfere. However, go to your little friend and she will tell you what is happening."

Quickly, Ahohiel ran through the woods and returned to the little tool shed behind Commander Estigan's house. He was rewarded only seconds later when Lora entered as well.

"Oh, I knew you would come back," she said as she hugged him. "I just knew it. I missed you."

"I missed you, too. I've thought about you a lot and I have been praying for you. Your sister?"

"She's here, just like you promised. What will happen next."

"Lora," he laughed. "I don't know everything that's going to happen next. Only God knows and he told me about your sister. Now God has sent me to you for help."

"How can I help?" she asked doubtfully.

"You have already helped. But here is what I want you to do. A friend of mine, a woman named Estella Edisni, was taken by the soldiers. Can you find out what has happened to her?"

She nodded her head and ran out of the shed. He marveled at her obedience and praised God for her.

When Estella was taken by the guards, she was led directly to the Commander's home. However, because they walked along the streets and Ahohiel ran the shorter route through the woods, he arrived first. She was led into Commander Estigan's den, and the guards waited in the outer room. Lora came into the room with drinks for the guards and sat down as she began to talk idly about her toys and sister and other such things. She could hear everything in the next room.

Commander Estigan sat at his desk and stared into Estella's face. She sat in the chair opposite him with her hands bound uncomfortably behind her. After a few moments, he arose and approached her, placing his hand on her belly.

"That's very odd. Don't you think so, my friend?"

"Commander Estigan," she said haughtily, "in the first place, you are not my friend. In the second place, I have no idea what you are talking about. I would kindly ask you to remove your hand from my body."

"Tut tut, my dear. Do let's try to work this out like friendly neighbors." She shivered as he moved his hand up and over her breasts. He smiled and walked back to his desk. He shook his head in mock wonder as he sat on the edge of the desk. "It's just that you've always been such a tiny thing and lately you've really begun to turn into a glutton. But, I suppose, that's fine. You don't seem to be putting on any weight."

He changed the subject. "Are you aware that my daughter has returned from Akadon. We've been so happy here lately."

"I'm very pleased for you!" she snapped. "I believe families should be together."

"True. That's true. So, tell me, have you had any interesting guests lately?"

"You know as well as I that those two strange men were at my home a few weeks ago. I promptly reported them. You lied to me and said you would work to bring my men home again. I should have known better than to believe a rodent like you."

He raised his hand threateningly near her face and lowered it again. "You had best watch your mouth, neighbor," he hissed. "I have no problem at all having you locked up with an unattended broken jaw."

She raised her head proudly. "You can knock my head off. I have no fear of you anymore."

Poking his finger in her face, he asked her, "Tell me the truth for your own sake. Where is the other intruder?"

She suddenly looked surprised and nearly convinced him of her innocence. Shaking her head, she answered, "Is that what this is about? You know I came to you. You captured both men and took them to the prison on Leetra. I don't understand what you want of me."

His fist crunched into her cheek. She screamed in pain as blood spewed from her mouth.

"You are a liar!" he screamed. "I want the truth now! I am certain there is a third man, and he has been in your house since the arrest. I'll admit I was confused at first, but I did not want to overreact. However, now I know the second man we arrested does not answer the description at all of the man entering your house." Hs face was red with rage, but he quietly proceeded back to his chair. "I will give you the opportunity to tell me everything you know." He waited for a few seconds. "Don't you have two boys on one of the other islands? Let's see. Oh, yes. Now I recall. Peter and Maurice. Is that right?" She was fearfully shaking her head. "No? Oh, yes, I'm sure of it. You were recently given a promise that we would try to reunite you with some of your family." He clapped his hands twice and smiled. "Now I offer you another promise. I will exchange the life of this vagabond for the life of one of your sons." He stood up and moved around the desk. "I will have you locked up tonight. In the morning you must fill in the blank, so to speak. You will either help us find this man or you will tell me the name of your son you no longer hold dear. Guards!" he called out.

They hurried into the room and were instructed to secure her until morning. When Lora heard her father strike Estella, she had excused herself from the guards and hurried to Ahohiel. She quickly told him what she had heard.

"Little darling," he said. "Can you do one more thing? Get a message to her that neither God nor myself will desert her. Can you do that?" She sped away.

When she entered the room, her father was still in the den and the two guards were escorting Estella toward the front door. There was a large bruise on her cheek. Lora quickly snatched a wet towel from the serving tray she'd carried in earlier.

"Uh oh," she said innocently. "You got hurt. Here, let me wipe it." The guards were used to Lora's childish ways and knew her father usually spoiled her, so they didn't stop her. Estella's mind had gone blank with fear and pain and she absent-mindedly leaned over towards Lora, forgetting that Ahohiel had spoken of her earlier. "I have something to make you feel better," she whispered so the guards could not hear. She held the damp cloth on Estella's cheek for a moment and then whispered very quietly, "Our friend and our God will not leave us." Estella looked her in the eye. "Just keep praying."

Suddenly, Commander Estigan came into the room and took charge. "Lora! Leave that woman alone! Will you two get her out of here!" he yelled at the guards.

As soon as Lora had left Ahohiel, God had prompted him to flee into the woods again.

Lora went back to the bedroom where Regina sat on the edge of the bed arranging a vase of flowers. "Regina," she asked. "Can I talk to you?" Then she started bawling.

"Oh, honey!" she spun around on the bed and drew her little sister close. "What's wrong, baby? What's happened?"

"I have to talk with you," she sniffled.

A few minutes later when Regina came into his den, Commander Estigan sat nervously thumping his fist on the desk. He looked up when she walked in.

"I need to talk with you," she said as she sat down in the chair Estella had sat in a few minutes before.

"Not now, sweetheart," he said smiling. "I have a lot on my mind."

"Then I will talk at you," she said firmly as she leaned forward. As she did so, her hand slid along the arm of the chair into Estella's spattered blood, and she realized her hand had become bloody. She gazed at her hand for a moment and then closed it into a fist as though clutching something valuable.

"I really have no time to speak with you right now," he insisted.

She stood up. "Well then, I guess I will return to Akadon without even your goodbye."

He motioned for her to sit down. "I do not understand this foolishness."

"It is your foolishness which is beyond my comprehension," she said without taking a seat. "I realize you are afraid."

He scowled at her. "I am not afraid of anything."

"Father." She smiled as she sat down. "You are afraid of your own shadow. You are afraid of this stranger that is among us. You are afraid of what Lora has been saying about my release. Do you have a better reason for my being set free other than God's intervention? You are afraid of that woman you beat up when she couldn't even defend herself. You are, of course, mostly afraid of that old man."

"It's not good to call him that. That name makes him very angry."

She looked around. "There's no one here but you and me. Are you going to report me? Why don't you arrest me or beat me up like that other woman?" She opened her hand and smeared the blood across the reports on his desk.

"Why are you doing this?" he snapped.

"I should ask you the same."

"I am doing my job of keeping this area secure."

She laughed and stood up. "Oh yes, we must keep Afeena secure. God forbid that a man should be roaming around free on the island. God only knows what could happen."

"What has gotten into you?" he screamed. "I will not put up with this attitude."

Suddenly she kicked over a standing ashtray, dumping its contents onto the carpet. But she remained in control of her voice. "I said you ought to arrest me."

"I am not going to arrest my daughter. However, you will clean up this mess and change your attitude or you shall be locked in your room. Why are you acting like this?"

Her lower lip started to quiver. "Because I love you. Or at least, once I loved you. Are you so stupid? My father is a Village Commander. As his daughter, I ought to have been treated with respect on Akadon, if there was even a need for having been there. I know I was sent there to keep you living in fear. Instead of being treated with respect, I was the lowest servant scraping scum from the bathroom floor. I knew at any time if you screwed up, my life could be in danger. I saw other people beaten for some nonsense that some other person supposedly did. I have been beaten." At that she turned and hoisted her dress to her shoulder to reveal bright red scars. She turned and looked back at him again. "If I am going to be treated like an enemy, then I intend to act like an enemy. I will no longer stand by like some cow waiting for some man's pleasure." He stood up, surprised, and started to approach her. "Yes, father, I was raped. Not once, by one lackey, but whenever someone felt the urge." She grabbed a poker from the fireplace and waved it toward him.

"Darling, I'm your father. I never knew," he begged compassionately. "Please, let's make up and work through this."

"No!" She yelled as she continued to wave the poker around. "What would you have done if you had known? You would have felt angry and neither said nor done a thing."

He reached for the poker and she surprised him with a hard rap on his hand. He backed off.

"I have been treated like a slave, a dog, like a criminal, and I've done nothing wrong. My only crime is that I am the daughter of a stupid man!" She kicked over a small table with a lantern on it. "You can continue to be a servant to that old fool. You can continue to grovel at his feet. I am now an enemy and I am declaring war against you and Coracus!"

All this time she proceeded about the room and he followed her at a distance, hoping she would either settle down or he would have a chance to subdue her. Suddenly, she picked up another lantern which was burning and heaved it beyond his desk into the curtains. It cracked into the wall and the curtains burst into flame. As she was distracted by the flames for a moment, he flew over the chair she had been sitting in with his fist extended and knocked her cold.

"Now that's enough of this nonsense," he said as he stooped beside her. He slapped her lightly on the cheek in an effort to revive her. She did not respond. He was sure she was dead.

Chapter 12

"Well, if one must be a prisoner," Mashua commented as he sipped his drink, "this is certainly the way to do it." They sat before a banqueting table which Lanao had laid out for them and the other prisoners under his care. In all, there were over sixty prisoners and a dozen guards. During the last few days, every one of the prisoners and guards had either come to know the Lord or, at least, learned to respect those who did.

Mashua and Idiptu, though they were still confined to the prison building, were allowed to roam freely. They actually had more liberty than the guards who still maintained their posts, as the Denarites assisted Lanao and prayed with everyone who wanted prayer.

Rations were still scanty as Lanao had only a meager budget to purchase provisions. However, he and the other guards had begun to spend their own money to feed the prisoners. Lanao's family lived on Leetra, but he could only see them irregularly since they lived on the other side of the island and Lanao and his staff were quartered permanently at the prison. Therefore, he was especially pleased as his wife Cella and two adult sons were supposed to visit on this day. They had been to the prison before but had never been allowed beyond the outer lobby and yard. He had prepared this big feast to celebrate their visit and meeting his new friends. As the tables were being prepared, one of his guards informed him that his family had arrived.

"Mashua! Idiptu!" he called out. "Please come. There's someone I want you to meet." He didn't wait for them but hurried into the next room. Both of Lanao's sons were there, but their faces were one of grief and despair.

"Climus. Acton. What is wrong?"

Climus, the elder of the two, addressed him. "It's mother. She was feeling ill today, so we could hardly convince her to come." Lanao glanced around for her. "She said she couldn't come in," he explained. "We left her lying outside in the shade of a tree. Please come." They turned for the outer door and he added, "Father, I don't know how much longer she will last. She keeps getting worse."

"I know," he said. "I know." Just then, Mashua and Idiptu entered the room. "Oh, my friends." He quickly introduced everyone. "My wife Cella is outside. Let me explain. She has some disease, which many have gotten, and it has caused her flesh to turn very dark, and a great dizziness and fatigue often come upon her. She's had this for several years. It comes and goes. But each time it grows worse."

"It worries me greatly as so many have died," said Climus. "I am certain she does not have the strength to return home. She'll have to stay here until she feels better."

"Perhaps," Lanao said to Mashua and Idiptu, "you could go out and pray for her."

Idiptu smiled and nudged Mashua. "Hey, we get to go outside. Didn't we pray about that?"

"Please come." Lanao led everyone outdoors.

Outside, it was a warm and breezy day. It had rained a little that morning and helped to cool things off some. There was a dirt road running in front of the prison building. The area on the prison side was completely barren, except for a few clumps of grass. However, across the road was a small grove of trees and a field of wildflowers. The men quickly proceeded across the road to where Lanao's sons led.

An elderly woman lay in the shade of the trees. She had, as had been described, a sickly darkness all over her exposed flesh. Only a very shallow breath escaped from her, the only indication she was even alive. Lanao knelt beside her. She appeared to Mashua and Idiptu to be old enough to be his mother as he leaned close to her face.

"I am here now, Cella. I have brought some friends. They understand the problem, and they are men of God and want to pray for you."

She opened her mouth to speak, but only a long sigh escaped. Lanao moved aside and motioned to them. Mashua and Idiptu knelt on opposite sides of her and began to silently pray. After a few moments, Mashua placed one hand on her forehead and raised the other into the air.

"Almighty God!" he called out. "I thank you for your grace and for Lanao's faith in Cella's healing. Father, I do not know what caused this problem and know only a little about it, but I don't need to know. You know. You have allowed this so that your glory may be revealed. In the name of the Almighty God, be healed!" He waited for just a moment. "Thank you, Father." Both the men stood up and watched her. She opened her eyes and first saw Lanao.

"Oh, husband," she said bearing a large grin. "Oh, Lanao, it is so wonderful. I feel so good and can hardly stand it." She reached for him, and he extended a hand to help her up. Instead, she drew him to her and kissed him. Then, she sat up and hugged him. She began crying. Already, her skin was growing lighter in color and she seemed to grow younger before their eyes. "Oh, Lanao, what can I do? This feeling is so awesome. I feel like dancing or running."

"Well," he nodded toward Mashua and Idiptu, "you could thank them."

"Thank us," Mashua answered as he shrugged his shoulders, "for what? We merely said some words. We have no power to do something like this. You had better thank God."

Lanao and Cella stood up and hugged both men. "I am thankful," she said. "I do not know God, but if he can do these things," she spun around, "I will thank him and do whatever he asks."

Climus and Acton had watched this transformation first with doubt and then with amazement. As the others turned to go back into the prison, Climus spoke to his father. "We have an errand we must run. I'll tell you more later. You both go ahead and enjoy yourselves, and we shall return in an hour or so."

"But what is it, son?" he asked.

"Just trust me, Father. We'll be back soon."

They did have a party. Cella was the only woman present, but she didn't let that hold her back. As the men chanted songs they knew and Mashua and Idiptu taught them a few more, she tried to dance with every man there. Lanao watched her in total amazement.

"For almost thirty years we have been together," he told Mashua. "I married her for her cooking and because she would have me. No one else would have a drinker like me. Then, a few years ago, this sickness came upon her. The last few years have gotten worse as Coracus made our lives miserable. I have scarcely been allowed to leave here, and she could hardly ever leave home to come here. Now, look at her. She has more energy than when we met. I am afraid," he added thoughtfully, "she may seek a younger man."

"Have you ever been unfaithful?" he asked.

"Never. Though this type of deceit is rampant and I had a few opportunities, I have always loved her and been true."

"She will remember this. I assure you. Just keep loving her. She promised to do what the Lord asked. Honoring her husband would be one of the greatest desires he would place upon her."

Sholl came up behind Lanao and whispered in his ear.

"Perhaps you should come with me," he said to Mashua. "My sons have returned, but there's some sort of commotion outside."

He and Mashua headed back outside to find Climus and Acton at the head of a group of several men.

"Father," Climus said as he approached his father and gave him a hug. He looked at Mashua. "Please forgive me, sir. When I saw what happened to my mother, I began to think of these other people needing help." He motioned to the crowd. "Can you do anything for them?"

Mashua looked over the two dozen men gathered there. He could tell some were missing limbs or were lame. Some bore a similar complexion that Cella had earlier. One man stumbled around muttering nonsense to everyone. Mashua took a deep breath and realized Idiptu had joined him.

Chapter 13

Commander Estigan looked up from where he stooped next to his daughter. He was still stunned. He briefly glanced about the room. The fire beside his desk was burning itself out. The room was a shamble, but he barely noticed any of this. He wondered why she had carried on so. He heard a noise at the doorway and his wife entered, carrying Lora protectively. When she saw the blank and shattered expression on his face, she nervously back away a few paces.

"What have you done?" she asked. "What have you done here?"

He stood and made as though to approach her.

"No!" she screamed. "Leave us alone!" She ran from the room.

He could hear the bedroom door slam shut and the bolt slide in place. He went and tapped lightly on the door.

"Go away!" she yelled. "I am afraid of you. Just go away!"

He could hear Lora crying. He stumbled out into his backyard. "I didn't mean to do it," he said under his breath. He sat on a large stone under a tree. "What am I going to do?"

When the house seemed quiet, Lora and her mother cautiously left the bedroom and returned to the den. Squatting on the floor, nestling Regina's lifeless head in his lap, was

Ahohiel. He looked up as they entered. Tears filled his eyes. Lora ran to him and lay her head on his shoulder.

"Is this the man you've been seeing, Lora?" her mother asked.

She nodded her head.

"My daughter is dead," she went on. "If it could be possible, I would be willing to exchange my life for hers."

"That's enough of death," he said. "This one is still ours. We did not come here to cause destruction and death, but to give you your lives back." He leaned over and softly kissed the young girl's ear and whispered, "Regina, it's time to come back. Your mother and sister are here, and you still have things to do."

There seemed to be no response, but eventually Regina moved her arm and wrapped it around Ahohiel's back. Then she simply lay there motionless. Lora and her mother watched for several seconds until her mother called out nervously, "Regina, can you hear me?" A smile crossed the girl's lips. "Oh my, you're still alive."

Her mother ran to her and fell to her knees and began to cover Regina with kisses and caresses through her tears. Regina seemed baffled.

"Oh, mother, I have just had the most awesome dream. I saw a light and I ran toward it. Then, I was in the light and in a great and lovely garden. Then, a man approached me. He was so kind and gentle. We talked for a few minutes, but I don't remember what was said until he told me it wasn't time for me yet. I had to come back. He said I could not come in there until I fulfilled my duty here." She shook her head. "I really don't understand." She turned around and saw Ahohiel sitting behind her. "Who are you?"

He smiled. "Perhaps I am the one who is going to help you fulfill your duty."

"Do you know who I saw in my dream?"

He placed his hand on her cheek and she listened attentively. "First, it was not a dream. You had passed from this life. However, the Lord called me to your side. I believe you either saw one of God's holy angels or his anointed son. Whatever you saw, the message was from God. I do not know what he wants you to do but for this, accept the salvation that only he offers and become part of his family."

She glanced at her sister. "Like Lora?"

Ahohiel nodded. "Like Lora."

She took his hand. "I want that."

Her mother crept closer. "I also want this salvation." She clasped his other hand.

They heard a noise in the doorway, and everyone looked. Commander Estigan was standing there seething with anger. His eyes were narrowed with fury. "What are you doing in my house?" He brought both his fists over his head and stood there, not knowing what to say next.

Ahohiel looked back and forth at Regina and her mother. "Let's pray," he said quietly. "I'll lead and you both repeat after me."

Estigan started to raise his voice again. However, he felt constrained to do so and stomped out of the room.

Chapter 14

When the Rasomites had discovered the name of the castaway, what followed was a short period of mayhem as they all tried to explain that it was the letter he'd posted in Ifintim which had precipitated their failed voyage. He was totally confused and understood not a word. Eventually, Anam selected Crazon to spend time with him and share their experiences. John had taken them to a cave in the interior of the island and indifferently allowed them to move in. The language sessions went slowly and laboriously as the first thing Crazon learned was that his tongue had a scar gashed across it that had happened during one of his confinements. However, in the course of their time together, she prayed for him and he both accepted God as savior and his tongue was made whole. He had fled Afeena with his crew nearly two years before, when the island had been overrun by Coracus' and Daga's army. Their hope had been to escape to Dernay, as that was the name of this tiny island, and prepare for a counterattack later on.

However, their plans were cut short when they came under attack by nearly all of Coracus' navy. Their ship, The Farragan, received many blows and sank near Dernay. John did not know if any of his men survived as he had gone down with his ship and ordered them to escape with lifeboats. He had seen no other people since his landing and had, of course, never seen a dark-skinned person like a Rasomite.

When he had first seen them, he was certain he was hallucinating. Then, he was afraid they could be from his mortal enemy, Coracus.

He had no supplies. His weakened condition made it difficult to hunt or fish. As the days went by, however, the Rasomites were able to feed him well, and his health repaired quickly.

Crazon had explained to him in the beginning how their tiny craft had sunk in the storm. However, after about a week, she explained to him exactly how they had come ashore. They had assumed the boat to be lost in the storm and had never gone back looking for it.

He became very excited to immediately search for the craft. As the others were out hunting and roaming about the island, Crazon and John returned to where they had come ashore. They spent nearly an hour walking up and down the beach and gazing out to the sea beyond the rocks to see if the capsized boat might have washed up. Finally, he wanted to return to the exact spot they had last seen the boat.

Wading out to the point where they had rescued Zoana, the boat was discovered exactly as it had been left. It lay, bottom side up, mostly submerged in water. He tried to move it, but it had not only become waterlogged but had begun to sink into the sand. It wouldn't budge even with both them attempting to rock it.

He stood there with his hand on his forehead for a minute, thinking. "Tomorrow night," he said. "Maybe tomorrow night."

Crazon and John were excited to get back and tell them of their find. Later, all five of them attempted to move the boat to no avail. They could rock it back and forth and lift either end a couple of inches but could come nowhere near lifting it from the water. Anam explained to John that even if they were able to extract it from where it lay partly submerged, they could not possibly get it back to shore. He recalled how heavy it had been to drag from the bushes back on Afeena. Now, waterlogged and filled with silt, he doubted if they could even extract it from the water. Then, carrying it the half mile through a rocky barrier would have been impossible for twenty strong men.

"Tomorrow night," John said. "We'll try tomorrow night." He shot a knowing smile at Crazon with whom he had shared his plan.

The next evening, Anam was even more confused. Due to the incoming tide, the boat was completely submerged. However, they were now able to hoist each end of the boat a few inches toward the surface as they alternately piled rocks under each end of the boat and slowly raised it until the bottom broke through the surface. The boat seemed much lighter underwater than it had earlier. Anam began to understand John's thinking. They continued to lift it and support it with boulders until they could move it no more.

John saw the concern on Anam's face as he wondered what would be done next.

"Do not worry," John said. "One week, maybe less."

Everyone was tired and slept well that night. During the week they had lived there and been sharing John's cave, they had tried to make it more livable. They had laid a bed of leaves and grass down to make sleeping more comfortable. They had utilized the abundant grove of plum trees and discovered a host of edible roots and other plants. It was easy for them to snatch a fish from the water or capture a bird. John was enormously pleased with his new friends and began to put on weight as he grew healthier by the day.

Several times, they had returned to the lookout point where they had met. This point faced Akadon, which usually was clearly visible about five miles away. John explained that no one was interested in Dernay. It was simply a large, sandy rock in the sea, surrounded on all sides by either a rocky barrier or submerged reefs. He had seen few ships during his stay there and none had ever approached the island. The seaports of all three main islands were on the south side of the Isles. He had given up hope of ever being rescued. Besides, he had no interest in leaving Dernay before because he knew all the islands were occupied, and he would either be executed or spend the rest of his life in a cell. He had decided to live out his days in exile. However, now he felt the situation seemed to be changing. Even though the Rasomites could verify nothing for certain, he was sure there would be friendly forces all over the islands if he could secretly return and organize them. His name meant a lot to the people as he had repeatedly put his life on the line before Coracus.

No one else bothered to, but several times a day John would go out and check the boat. One morning he had risen early and left, returning just as the others were awakening.

"Come quickly!" he yelled. There was a smile on his face, and he was obviously excited.

They all ran to the water and soon saw his reasoning. The tide was coming in. Reaching the boat in water over their waists it was an easy thing to roll the boat, now almost completely dried out, right side up into the water. In a few minutes, as the water continued to rise, now nearly to their chests, they began to maneuver the craft through the maze of rocks. Soon they had dragged the boat ashore and rolled it onto its side to finish drying out.

John climbed inside the lower part of the boat and began inspecting it. He came out a few minutes later. "It is full of dirt and sand. Many holes. One dangerous crack along the bottom. But I will fix all that."

"And then what?" Anam asked him.

John threw his arms into the air with glee. "Then we will attack Akadon!" He disappeared back into the boat. When he came back out, the others were relaxing in the sun. "This is not a very good boat." He shook his head incredulously. "You came all the way from Ifintim?"

Anam nodded. "Yes. All the way, with God's help. John, the ones who built this had not even seen a boat in twenty years. They had no plans or directions except from books. The books spoke of things they knew nothing about."

"I see. Then I am sorry for what I said. Knowing this, it's an excellent craft. I am sure in a couple of days it can be made ready."

Chapter 15

No one had heard anything of Coracus since he had supposedly drowned with all hands on the way to Leetra. Except for his brief visit at Lanao's prison, he had disappeared. Lanao had thought of him several times, but he was still afraid of the man and his threats, so he decided to leave well enough alone and told no one.

The day Coracus had left the prison it was still raining, and he had departed with no guard. The same day, the crew from a second boat (it was obvious to Lanao to be the same one which had rescued Coracus) had all been found together brutally slaughtered. A search had been made for the perpetrators as it was assumed by many to be rebels against the government. Of course, nothing was found. So, it was entirely possible that Lanao and his two friends were the only ones who knew Coracus still lived.

Lanao had heard of Daga's ascension to the throne and that it had been done with little turmoil. Everyone had expected a massive purging, especially among those in the palace on Akadon. However, the news Lanao heard was that no one had yet lost their lives. No one had even been imprisoned as Lanao would know that soon enough. There had been some mild reshuffling of responsibilities among the leadership. A few had lost their posts. It appeared that Daga's reign would be much kinder than his predecessor.

However, there was this gnawing fear inside Lanao, which he guarded from everyone, that something awful was about to happen. He suspected Daga would suddenly unleash his fury once he knew who was truly loyal to him. He also thought Coracus would suddenly make his appearance and seek revenge on everyone, the usurper of his throne first.

To Mashua's question of Coracus' whereabouts, he gave an evasive answer, which was true, that no one knew where the Emperor was. He said he preferred not to discuss it, so the matter never came up again. He did, however, wrestle in his mind constantly as to what he ought to do with his secret. Finally, he could stand it no more and determined to report to Daga and inform him. He felt it would be fairly easy for someone of his status to speak with the new Emperor. He called Sholl into his office.

"Sholl, I have been thinking about my prisoners ever since Daga assumed control. It appears that he is mostly seeking to maintain the status quo and spread a little goodwill Though I am not so stupid as to believe Daga is kind and generous, I am hoping he desires to be fair. It is my intent to gain an audience with him and petition him for more freedom for these men."

Sholl laughed. "More freedom? Most of them already have more freedom than we do except, of course, they cannot leave. However," he added more seriously, "I completely concur with and understand your thoughts. What do you expect will happen to the two from Ifintim?"

Lanao shrugged. "I don't know. I am quite surprised that no one out of this prison seems much interested in what we've been doing. You know Climus and Acton have been all over the island telling everyone. Them and those folks our friends healed."

Sholl nodded.

"That is," Lanao corrected himself, "the ones God healed."

"So, when do you intend to leave?"

"As soon as possible. Of course, I can't simply jump on a ship and head out, but I'll go down to the bay this morning and have a message sent personally of my desire to go."

"And while you are gone?"

"I place my trusted assistant in charge. You know what I would do if I were here."

Sholl looked bewildered. "Sir, I am no longer sure what you would do if you were here."

"Well, the prisoners know what's expected." He laughed. "If you have any questions just ask them."

"Yes, sir. And what of Mashua and Idiptu? Any special requests?"

"Treat them well." Lanao shook his head and leaned back in his chair. "I don't know why we are talking like this. I know neither if I shall go to Akadon or, if so, when I'll go." He stood up. "I am going down to the docks now. I should be back in an hour or so." They shook hands and he left.

Sholl leaned back in his chair. He thought of sitting at Lanao's desk, but couldn't quite bring himself to that just yet. On a few occasions, he had been placed in charge before when Lanao needed a break and went to see his family. But he knew things were different now. Before, he had always been afraid that something terrible would happen. Some demand from Coracus would send everyone scurrying. Or there would be a fight among the prisoners that he would have to subdue. However, he recalled nothing of a serious nature had ever happened. He took a deep breath and was pleased that things would probably be even better now. He felt free to lower his guard.

He got up and strolled the corridors of the prison for a few minutes. Most of the prisoners were out of their cells and either in the big hall now used for relaxing and games or just standing around talking.

"Sholl!" a guard called out from the end of the corridor. He snapped out of his reverie and hurried to him. "There is a strange man in the outer lobby who wished to speak with Lanao. I told him Lanao was gone and he asked for you."

"Who could he be?" he asked as they walked back to the front.

The guard merely shrugged his shoulders. "I don't know, sir. He said he had come not too long ago and spoke with Lanao about something and now he wants you to finish the job."

Sholl scratched his chin. "I don't know of any unfinished projects. Lanao told me nothing of any visitors."

The guard unlocked the inner door that led to the lobby and Sholl entered. He saw what looked like a beggar sitting on the old wooden bench. His clothing was old and ragged. The hood on his shirt was pulled over his face. The old man's back seemed to be bent out of shape as he stooped over.

The guard asked Sholl if he should remain behind.

Sholl fingered his sword and his dagger. "No, I'll be fine."

"I will stay within shouting distance inside if you need anything." He pointed to the entrance. "Both the door and the gate on the fence are secure." The guard left Sholl with the stranger.

Sholl remained standing and kept several paces between himself and the stranger. "How may I help you?"

"Where is your master?" he asked with a deep, rasping voice. "I really needed him."

Sholl spoke firmly. "The guard said you had talked with the magistrate recently. However, he told me nothing of any meetings, and he tells me everything."

"Everything?"

"He tells me everything. We have no secrets."

"However, he did not tell you I had visited him?"

Sholl was becoming frustrated. "He told me of no meetings. Now, I must demand, who are you?"

The stranger sat up straight now. "Perhaps the old warden was more faithful than I suspected."

"I do not understand. Who are you?"

He threw his hood back. Though he had grown a scraggly beard and looked very fatigued, Sholl recognized Coracus immediately.

"Majesty!" he exclaimed as he sank to one knee and lowered his head.

Coracus stood up and walked over to Sholl. "Now tell me," he said calmly, "where is your master?"

Sholl looked up at Coracus. "I am sorry, your highness. Everyone thought you had perished in the storm. Daga has assumed your throne. Lanao is planning to go to him seeking advice on the prisoners." He lowered his head again. Suddenly, it dawned on him the true reason Lanao could be headed for Daga. He looked back up, and Coracus' knife blade pierced Sholl's uniform from behind and entered his heart. Sholl crumbled to the floor.

Coracus shook his head. "Well, I guess I judged your master properly after all. You, however, remained true to the end. I know you shall keep our secret." He stooped down over Sholl and touched his chest. "Does that hurt?"

Sholl had remained silent but gasped, "Yes."

"Let me help you." He pulled his dagger from Sholl's back and slit the man's throat.

Sholl collapsed the rest of the way to the floor in a pool of blood. Coracus reached into Sholl's cape and quietly pulled out the keys.

"You have been very honorable. I know you shall keep my secret. I shall let myself out."

Coracus quickly opened the door and proceeded to the gate. A voice called out for him to halt, but before the guard could further respond, he had opened the gate and ran off.

Chapter 16

Lanao was nervous, but very pleased with himself. He rested on a ship bound for Akadon. Having approached the captain of the dock with his verbal request, he'd expected to be asked to put it in writing, which he would have done on the spot. However, the captain's response was to have him quickly board the ship, which he was now on, and set sail for Akadon immediately. He'd sent a message back to Sholl of his success in securing passage.

It was a beautiful day. He leaned back on the chair, which had been placed on deck just for him, and felt the salty sea breeze blowing through his hair, certain God himself had gone before him and made all the arrangements. He hoped his words to Daga would be accepted as easily as those to the captain had been.

"Are you enjoying the trip, sir?" came a voice from behind him.

"Oh yes. I never expected to be traveling today," he said without looking around. "Things seem to be going much more smoothly lately. Don't you think?"

He received no answer and looked over his shoulder, right into the Emperor's face.

"Surprised, my friend?" Coracus displayed an evil, toothy grin. "Don't call out. I have a knife against your back." Lanao could feel the pressure. "You have severely hurt my feelings because I thought I could trust you. And you maintained your silence for such a long time. That's impressive. Do you know, you are the only surviving person who knows I still live? You and those two prisoners. They shall not survive long, either."

"How do you know I didn't tell everyone?"

"Your closest confidant didn't even know we had spoken."

"Then Sholl knows you are still alive?"

"He knew," he chuckled. "However, he will keep a secret better than you."

Lanao felt the prick of the dagger in his back. "You have slain him then, you…"

The knife slide in so easily. Lanao slumped in his chair and attempted to call out, but suddenly his mind went dark and he fell to the floor. He was instantly surrounded by members of the crew who had been working only a few feet away. Coracus was gone. The crew members tried to help him back to his seat, figuring that he was merely nauseated from the voyage before they realized he had been stabbed.

"Quickly, search the ship. There was an old man talking with him," called out one of the crew members.

There was no doctor on board, but the captain was summoned immediately. By then, they had removed most of Lanao's clothing and were cleaning the wound with sea water.

The man who had seen the one conversing with Lanao described him to the captain as best as he could. "He was an older man who seemed to have a stooped back. He was wearing rags and had a few days growth of beard."

"I allowed no one aboard answering a description like that. I want every inch of this ship searched before we reach Getz. We shall be there within an hour. No one will go ashore until this assailant is found."

The ship was searched thoroughly, but when Akadon came into view, the mysterious assailant still had not been discovered.

"We must take Lanao ashore," the captain decided. "If he doesn't get medical help very soon, we will lose him. I will go ashore with only two rowers. Everyone else will remain here and continue to search."

"Lanao, old friend, can you hear me?"

Lanao opened his eyes to see an old man sitting beside the bed where he lay. Despite that he found it hard to focus, he immediately recognized his old friend Shapel. His attempt to move produced a stab of pain through his back and chest.

Shapel laid a hand on his shoulder. "No. No. You won't be moving for a while. Just relax. The blade went into your back and nearly pierced clear through."

Lanao settled back into the bed and suddenly remembered the urgency of his mission. "No, Shapel. It is absolutely imperative that I see Daga now."

"See the Emperor? That's what the captain said. Something about caring for your prisoners. What's going on, Lanao?"

"I cannot say just yet. However, lives are in danger the longer I wait."

"But, Lanao, you are neither fit to travel nor to present yourself before the Emperor."

Lanao glanced around the room. From the appearance of the shelves of medication and rolls of gauze and bandage, he was obviously in a doctor's office.

"How did I come here?"

"The ship's captain brought you. He said you had been stabbed, which you were. He brought you here himself."

Lanao smiled at Shapel and shook his head. "You are not going to trick me into believing you are a doctor, are you?"

Shapel laughed. "Why not? I was a carpenter for years. There is not that much difference. Now I repair broken bodies instead of broken furniture. What's the difference between a broken chair leg and your leg?"

"A chair leg does not shed as much blood nor will it cause me to shriek in pain if you chisel on it." He laughed aloud and then, feeling the pain, wished he hadn't.

"It's been five years, Lanao. We've a lot of catching up to do. How's Cella?"

"The last time I saw her, she was dancing."

"Cella? No, never."

"Shapel, I would love to chat, but I really must go. How far is the palace?"

Shapel sighed. "We are on the wharf. The palace is still in the same place, of course, only a quarter mile from here. Lanao, you are still my patient, and I advise you to stay in bed at least a day or so."

"Shapel, shut up! Do you know nothing at all? Can you not see that I was just attacked? My assailant may be going for Daga next. When this happens, will you still be babbling your stupid advice? Now, you must help me to the fullest extent possible to get into the palace."

"Of course," he said. "Of course. There is no other way than to walk." He helped Lanao sit up in bed. "Do you feel up to it?"

"No. But I have no choice. I must be up to it. Tell me if you can. The ship I sailed on, is it still in the bay or has it pulled to shore?"

Shapel went and glanced out of his window. "Aye, it's still out there."

Shapel helped Lanao up and they left the office, securing the door as they left. It had been several years since Lanao had been to Akadon, and he would have liked to have looked about and took in the sights. However, the urgency of his mission and the great pain he felt caused him to totally refocus his thoughts. They passed several people, some of whom spoke briefly to them, but he offered them none of his time.

Finally, they reached the palace and were quickly admitted. The guard explained that Emperor Daga was busy with other affairs and it would be about an hour before he could see them.

Lanao pulled up his shirt to reveal several layers of heavy gauze which were soaked in fresh blood. "Do you see this wound? I will not tell the Emperor what to do, of course. However, I am here so he may avoid a similar fate. Would you please inform him of that?"

"Are you telling me," demanded the guard, "you are aware of a possible assassination attempt and that this visit does not pertain to your visitors on Leetra?"

"That is correct."

"Why, then, did you come here under false pretenses and not make this known earlier?"

Lanao grimaced as another wave of pain went through him. "Because," he forced himself, "I wanted to avoid this sort of situation."

"Perhaps," added Shapel, "you are the type that flaunts information like that, but it ought to be shrouded in secrecy. This man," he nodded toward his companion, "has risked his life to deliver this information."

"Of course, you are correct," he admitted. He quickly sent another messenger to Daga.

A few minutes later, Lanao and Shapel were escorted into a small conference room. Behind a large wooden table sat

Daga and his new chamberlain. Besides them, there was a guard at either end of the table. Lanao glanced at Daga as they entered the room and the door was shut. As Coracus' chamberlain, he had come to Leetra's prison many times to work on admissions from prisoners or to check on their status. Lanao had always been impressed by Daga's physique, despite his age. Now, however, his face was drawn in fatigue and his shoulders sagged. He leaned heavily on the table.

The chamberlain spoke sharply. "Bow before your leader!"

Shapel knelt to the floor and lowered his face. Lanao attempted to, but the pain in his chest forbade him. There was also a conviction in his heart that he should not.

Daga was interested. "Do not bow, warden," he said kindly. "I am informed that you were very recently injured. Please, take a seat."

Two large wooden chairs were slid away from the wall nearer the table for them by one of the guards. He then poured them each a large goblet of water from a pitcher sitting off to one side.

The chamberlain spoke. "You have been brought here to undergo questioning concerning any of your activities and any of your knowledge in an alleged assassination attempt on his royal majesty, Emperor Daga. I will be asking the questions and request you to restrict yourself to answers appropriate to the questions. Are you ready to begin?"

Lanao started to nod his head when Daga interrupted. "Lanao, let me begin by asking a question. Do you intend to cooperate with us or shall you guard your answers to protect yourself?"

"Your Majesty," he replied, "I expect to give a thorough review of everything I know. However, some of my answers may, uh, compromise what you suppose to be true."

Daga leaned back in his chair. "Unfortunately, as I've learned many times in the past, in situations like this that is usually true. Am I to believe persons that are close to me are involved?" He glanced about the room.

"Yes sir, but none of these."

"Then, since you are willing to cooperate fully, I believe we'll dispense with the regular questions. Go ahead and tell us everything you know."

"Let me begin by naming the, uh..."

"Villain!" chimed in Daga. "Go ahead. Who is the man? Do I know this person very well?"

"You know him very well, sir. He is Coracus."

Shapel had been idly sitting in his chair and sipping his water. When he heard Lanao's answer, he dropped his goblet on the stone floor. There was a hushed silence for several seconds. Lanao glanced at the two guards and the chamberlain. They were obviously shaken. However, Daga smiled and shook his head.

"That is why you came over here? Lanao, news must travel ever so slowly because transportation has become so weakened. My old friend Emperor Coracus drowned in the storm a few days ago. We had a wonderful memorial service for him here. We deeply regretted his loss, but we look forward to a prosperous future. Who else might have seen this assailant and could verify his identity?"

"The only ones who remain alive and saw him on the morning he reached my prison are the two men from Ifintim."

"I have heard of these two. I would love to converse with them. Are they interesting people?"

"I would guarantee, your Majesty, an encounter with them can change a man's life."

"Ah yes. However, I feel it odd that only you have seen this man and are so certain of his identity. Are you certain that no one else has seen him? How can you be sure?"

"Several others have seen him, sire."

"But you said…" he trailed off.

"I said I am the only survivor. Are you aware that on the morning his boat sank there was another boat?"

Daga looked at his chamberlain. "Perhaps you were right and we should have restricted it to just questions. Now I am being questioned."

He looked back at Lanao and rolled his eyes back. "Yes, warden, I was told there was a second boat. However, someone confused relayed the information as I know for certain the boat you are referring to arrived several hours before the Emperor's boat was scheduled to arrive. But," he waved his hand, "continue your story."

"Coracus arrived at my prison on schedule that morning. He was accompanied by one guard and admitted as a prisoner to join the other two men I mentioned. We had him for only a few minutes. When I discovered his identity, he soon left."

Daga chuckled. "Why would you wait for three weeks to deliver this information?"

"Because, sire, Coracus, as the Emperor over the Isles of Aboti, swore me to secrecy. I have feared for my life since that morning."

"And why have you come now?"

Lanao sighed as his breathing was very labored. "Because your life is more important than mine. I wanted to spare your life."

"Let us suppose Coracus lives. Why do you think he would come after me? Have I done anything wrong? I have not rejoiced in his death."

"Coracus does live, sire. I came here because I could no longer stand the burden of secrecy."

"You said you feared for your life. Did he give you a reason to fear?"

"When I spoke with him, I could see his anger at my discovery. I believe you are aware Emperor Coracus does not stay angry for long before going after revenge. Also, the morning he was in my prison, the entire crew of that second boat was ruthlessly slaughtered."

"There were, I believe, five men on that boat. How could anyone, even that man, pull off a murder like that? Did he sneak up and surround them or something?" Daga and the chamberlain laughed.

Lanao remained serious. "Your Majesty, I have seen how the Emperor operates. For example, there are five men, besides yourself, gathered here. If you wanted us all silenced permanently how could it be done? I use this merely as an example and not meaning to be insulting. Could you not have the guards kill each of myself and the doctor? Then have the chamberlain slay the guards? Now you face only one opponent. If you gave the order, who would oppose you?"

Daga sat nervously back in his chair and considered this. "But why would Coracus wait so long before making himself known?"

"I don't know that, sire."

Daga nodded. "No one else has seen him, though?"

"Yes, sir, my assistant on Leetra has apparently seen him."

"And when was that?"

"Shortly after I left the prison to depart for here, your Majesty."

"Uh, warden, how could you possibly know if he saw Coracus after you left?"

"Because just before he stabbed me en route to here, he told me so. He also told me he slew him."

"When was the last time you saw this man?"

"Less than two hours ago, when he put a dagger in my back."

"Is that ship still in the bay?" Daga asked one of the guards.

The guard nervously shrugged his shoulders.

"Uh, your Majesty, if I may," spoke up Shapel, "it was still in the bay when we left my office on the wharf."

Daga wiggled his finger at the guard and then at the door. The guard left to determine the location of the ship.

"See that it stays out there until I figure this out!" he shouted as the guard left.

"I will admit," Daga addressed Lanao, "something very suspicious has happened." He nervously rapped his fingers on the table. "Do you have any more information or evidence to offer?" Lanao lifted his shirt to show his bloody gauze wrappings. "I see. Umm. I have no further questions for now." He looked at his chamberlain who shook his head. "You must stay close, warden, but you are permitted to leave."

All the men stood up from the table.

"With your Majesty's permission," said the doctor, "I will take him back to my office and apply new wrappings. He will be there if you should need him."

"Of course," Daga said as he massaged his jaw thoughtfully with one hand.

When Daga was back in his room he sat on a large, over-stuffed armchair and considered this dismal state of affairs. He was certain Lanao was correct. In fact, deep inside, he had felt from the very first that the wily Coracus had survived. It had gone too easy drowning that old fox. However, now that he was certain, he was shaken to the core of his being. He didn't even feel safe here in his room, which was not truly his if Coracus still lived.

He thought of his options. If he announced that Coracus lived and extended his greetings, he knew his own life would eventually be forfeit. Coracus, as the warden had suggested, always got even. If he announced that Coracus lived and ordered his capture as the villain he was, the entire realm would be in disarray. No one on the islands truly supported this evil man. However, Daga knew most would only associate himself as the lesser of two evils. Everyone would fear that if Coracus were to regain control of the throne, there would be a purge and he would not stop until everyone in the islands were dead. He briefly considered storming the ship. If he were still on the ship, Daga would order his immediate execution. The problem would be over. However, if he had somehow managed to escape the ship, this action would only make matters worse.

"Have you considered suicide?" came a voice from behind him.

He whirled around to the little settee which encircled the window behind him where Coracus sat, fingering the tip of his dagger.

"Please, don't get up." He played with the dagger as though to throw it. "I like you in this position."

"Excellency! You're alive!"

"Skip the further deceit and we'll go right to the point."

"How did you get in here, sire?"

The old man cackled. "Daga, my true friend, I know methods in and out of this palace that even you do not know about."

"Then you know I betrayed you? I have felt awful for this whole time."

"I am so sorry to hear that. Perhaps I can use that in your eulogy. Did you think I would die so easily?"

"I knew you would live. I have known it ever since the day you left."

"You should have used this wisdom before you betrayed me."

"How did you get back to shore? The warden from Leetra was quite sure that you were still on the ship."

Coracus cackled. "You cannot bind me. That stupid captain. I'll have him slain for bringing an assassin ashore. They placed a blanket over the center seat on the boat to lay the warden. When they went back to get him, I snuck onto the boat and hid under the blanket."

"You are slippery, aren't you."

"Enough of this chat. I have a lot of house cleaning to begin today."

It had been easier for Coracus to kill his other victims. They had more reverence for him. Though they feared him, no one ever expected to seriously meet his blade. Also, they were not used to seeing a man his age suddenly strike out like a snake. Daga knew those things to his advantage. He had no reverence for the villain, though he had sworn fidelity many times. He had seen Coracus as he would sit calmly engaged in a conversation without warning suddenly slash a man's neck and walk away.

When Coracus fell on Daga, he was prepared for the assault. He even allowed Coracus to nearly reach him, the better to throw him off-balance. Coracus had aimed for under Daga's left arm, into his ribs near his heart. As he leaned forward, Daga spun around, grabbed Coracus' knife arm and pulled him over the heavy chair. He brought his left fist down on the base of Coracus' neck. Coracus went limp.

"Guard!" he called out as he ran to the door. Three guards appeared in the doorway and Daga spun around to indicate where he had just subdued Coracus a moment before. The old fox had disappeared again.

Chapter 17

Anam awoke with a jolt. John was squatting before him with a smile upon his face. Anam glanced up and down at him, noting he had put on at least twenty pounds in the last three weeks. He looked so much younger. He no longer looked like a scrawny, old man.

"The boat is ready! Can we leave now?" he asked.

Anam glanced around at the still slumbering women. He looked out the cave door into the darkness.

"John, it's still night."

"It is nearly dawn. If we leave now, we can be there early. That is if we row hard and the wind is for us."

"Then you fixed the sail as you said you would? But it was really tore up. How could you fix it?"

"I used thread from the sail itself and carefully fixed every tear. It was a lot of work and I was up most of the night." He held up his hands by the firelight and showed how bloody they were from being poked so many times.

"I couldn't understand how you were going to fix that hull. The gap ran the whole length and was large enough to put my arm through."

John nodded. "I took planks from the upper part of the boat and not only repaired the crack but created another floor in case the first does not hold true. Granted, your boat now takes on the appearance of something more like a raft than a sea-faring vessel, but we have only to travel to Akadon. When we have taken control, I will once again have a grand ship and will be able to return you to Ifintim. Can we leave now?"

By now the three women were sitting up to listen to the conversation.

"Crazon," John said, moving toward her. "Come and see." He took her by the hand and led her toward the opening of the cave. "I've finished the boat. It's time to leave."

The boat was not as beautiful and polished as it had been when they departed Ifintim. However, when it started to grow light, each of the Rasomites crawled around the interior searching for possible leaks. They could find none. As John had said, the sail was only half the size of before but seemed quite adequate to get them to Akadon.

They all stood back looking it over, Anam with his hands on his hips. "Let's go. Let's get out of here."

"Let's pray first," Paluqua insisted. They all knelt in a circle on the sand.

"Dear God, thank you for sending these new friends to me and for rescuing me from this island and from myself," John began. "Now bring us quickly to Akadon that we may begin to set things right. Also, again, thank you that they taught me about you."

"Father," Anam prayed, "when we left Afeena, you knew it was not our plan to come here. We, in fact, weren't even certain this place existed. But you knew. You brought us safely here to find this man, John Dunley. Thank you for that. You're in charge, Lord. We keep finding that out. You're still in charge. If it's Akadon where you want us, bring us there safely. Thank you, God."

They all sat quietly for a few minutes and then slowly moved for the boat. It was incredibly easier to move now that it was thoroughly dry. It was even lighter than when they left Afeena.

Chapter 18

"Estella," whispered Ahohiel in the dark, basement prison.

"Ahohiel! Oh, I knew you would come," she said as she hurried to the cell door. "But how did you get in here?"

"Lora's father doesn't know what to do with me. I just led the rest of his family to the Lord." He smiled with pleasure. "My mere existence infuriates him. However, apparently, the Lord has told him to leave his hands off me. At least for now."

"Then he knows you're here?"

Ahohiel shrugged his shoulders. "He doesn't know where I am. I'm pretty sure he doesn't think I'd dare come in here." He could now see her bleeding lips and bruised cheek. "He hit you, didn't he?" She nodded as he slipped his hand through the tiny window in the doorway and cupped her chin in his palm. "Dear God, bear her up a little longer and teach her to rejoice in having to suffer for you." He thought how tender her lips seemed and quickly removed his hand. "Uh, sister, I have to go now. I am going to seek your release. Please, keep praying." And he was gone.

She went back, sat in the darkness, and began to pray. "God, I don't understand why I am here. I don't understand why there are evil men like Coracus and Daga and like this commander. But I know if these things had not come into my life, I would have never known you. Thank you for sending your servant, Ahohiel, and bringing you to Afeena and Mendoa. Lord, you need many more like him. I praise you for him and, yes, I praise you for placing me here. Thank you, dear God." She began to cry. "Oh God, I miss my family so much. Please bring us together quickly."

She sensed someone in the cell with her and opened her eyes. A man stood before her dressed in battle gear. He had a sword in one hand. For a moment she thought he might be one of the guards, but then she sensed both light and heat emanating from him.

"Who are you? Were you sent to harm me or to set me free?"

"Estella, you are already free, and I would never harm you but have been sent by the Almighty God to bless you and give you a message and a gift."

She fell on the floor in front of him. "Oh, whatever you are, I am hardly worthy to receive a gift from God."

He stooped down by her and took her hand. It was at once very strong and so very gentle, so much like Ahohiel's.

"My name is Orioni. I am the guardian angel of Anam and his people." She nodded. "You have been chosen to lead a revival in the village of Mendoa."

"But, sir," she waved one hand to indicate her cell, "I will do what I can, but I am just a woman. I know only of the Lord what your servant, Ahohiel, taught me. And I am locked in a cell."

"You will be free from here very soon. You will not do these works in your own strength but will have the sword of God." He handed her the sword. She grasped its handle tightly and looked it up and down. "Lastly, when you hear the news of your family, remember this is also the Lord's plan."

"I don't understand," she said.

"You will understand when these things are revealed."

He vanished so quickly as to surprise her. However, she then heard the clinking sound of her cell door being unlocked. The door swung open. But no one was there. Then, she heard the sound of the outer door at the top of the stairway being opened, which had been closed but not locked, and she quickly ran up the stairs toward it. As she did so, she realized the sword was gone. She stopped and looked at her hands in confusion. Though the sword was gone she still felt great strength as though she carried a weapon. She walked up to the outer cell door and saw that it was open. This did not completely surprise her as she knew the guards had left the outer door unlocked. However, she was still amazed at the inner door being unlocked in such an unusual manner. She walked out into the open by the street where was a bench with a covering over it. She sat down and waited.

Inside she was so giddy she didn't know what to do. First, she thought she should go hide in her own house. Then, she wanted to go find Ahohiel and tell him about the angel. Then she felt she should go to Commander Estigan's house and confront him again. She was so delighted now to know there were three other females who had also found God. She no longer felt alone.

Finally, she was confused again as she began to wonder where all the guards could be. She thought she should flee before they came back and locked her up again. However, then she knew that a prison door could no longer make her a captive. She headed for Commander Estigan's house.

She approached the house and timidly tapped at the door. There was no answer. She knocked harder and heard someone coming. A pretty, young, red-haired teenager answered the door. As soon as Regina saw Estella with still bloody lips and a bruised cheek, she knew who it must be.

"Praise God!" she called out. "So, father did set you free before he left."

Estella shook her head. "Your father did not release me, but the Lord." Then she smiled. "But I rejoice to hear you praise God. You must be Regina."

Regina opened the door and let Estella in. "Yes, come in. We were just cleaning house as we had a little argument here a while ago. Mother! Lora!" she called out. "We have a visitor." Her mother and Lora came from the den and were pleased to see her.

"Then you know what has happened to Ahohiel?" her mother asked.

"No," Estella asked nervously, "is something wrong?"

"We hope not," Regina said. "He came here a few minutes ago and turned himself in, offering himself as long as you were set free. However, even while they argued about this, the Island Commander's coach arrived, and father took three of his guards and Ahohiel back to Artuna."

"I truly wanted to see him, but I agree, this must be God's work. Will they be gone long?"

"Well," said their mother, "he told us that as long as all the trouble-makers were secure, Mendoa would not need him and he would probably be gone for the night."

"Wonderful!" exclaimed Estella. "We have a lot to do. First, I want to tell you what happened back in my prison cell and why I am here."

Commander Estigan reached his Commander's house by way of the coach in just a few minutes. He was escorted by several of his own and his commander's guards when he arrived at Borda's house. Borda himself was at the curbside when they arrived.

"Ah, Estigan," he said, helping him down. "It's so good to see you." Borda was a much larger man than his subordinate. "I was certain you would need some help. I felt it in my bones, you might say."

They shook hands. "As you say, I needed your help. Actually, this renegade I had already captured, but he is so sneaky I was afraid I would lose him. Your coach arrived at exactly the right moment."

Borda went to the side of the coach and looked in. Ahohiel was bound hand and foot with chains such that he would not be able to walk without stooping over. Running would be impossible.

"So, this is the trouble-maker. I knew there had to be more than two of them. I don't know if you are aware of it, but those other two I sent to the prison in Laytruce. Are you certain there are no more of these running around out there?"

"Quite certain, sir. This one had been hiding in one of the women's homes. She is also behind bars."

"Excellent! Was she pummeled at all?"

Estigan held up his right hand. "By my own hand, sir."

"Excellent! You have kept me wondering about you of late. I will keep this one here and send him to Akadon in the morning." Borda spoke to the driver and the guard still in the coach. "Take this one around back to the cell and have him locked up. I will attend to him in the morning." He glanced around at the other guards. "Then the rest of you are dismissed to return to your posts or back to Mendoa." He turned back to Estigan. "If you feel things are secure in Mendoa, I extend my home's hospitality for the night."

"I had hoped to be so invited," he said. "It would be a relief to be out of that household of women for a change."

"Ah yes, I had nearly forgotten. Your elder daughter has returned. I expect you two have had many tender moments together. Come, let's go inside."

Chapter 19

Idiptu and Mashua were surprised that Lanao had left and said nothing to them, not even a prayer request. In fact, at first, no one knew where Lanao had gone. The guards knew he had left and placed Sholl in charge but assumed he was spending the day at home. As soon as Sholl was found dead, a messenger was sent by horse to Lanao's home. However, he returned two hours later and said Lanao had not been home and they did not expect him. By this time, one of the other men had assumed control and sent a message to the Island Commander, Commander Ichvain, whose home and office were in nearby Laytruce where the docks were. The runner was told not to fill him in on the details so as not to spread alarm, but only that his presence was needed urgently at the prison. Unfortunately, Ichvain was out of his office when the messenger arrived at his home, out of breath.

When the commander finally returned, he left with the messenger and an associate immediately. Bertrane, the guard who had assumed authority was at his wits end by the time Commander Ichvain and the others arrived. They were escorted immediately to Lanao's office.

"Sir," Bertrane addressed the Commander as sweat formed on his brow, "first I want to apologize for my state of mind, but have you been made at all aware of what has happened here?"

The Commander shook his head calmly. "I have no idea what is going on. But I came as soon as I heard I was needed. It's been some time since I've been here, but then Lanao always kept things under control, and I have been very involved in other projects."

"Sir, Lanao left here earlier today. He had a meeting with Sholl, who you knew, before he left. No one knows where he has gone."

"Lanao has gone to Akadon to negotiate with Emperor Daga concerning the fate of his prisoners. However, I know he sent a messenger back. But, what do you mean, I knew Sholl? Where is Sholl?"

"Sir, for whatever reason the message was never received. Sholl has been murdered."

Suddenly Commander Ichvain grew very excited. "Sholl? Murdered? By whom? What is going on here?"

"Sir, one of the guards admitted a visitor today in the outer lobby. He came to see Lanao concerning a matter they had discussed earlier. As Lanao was gone, Sholl spoke with him. The guard thought he should remain, but Sholl wanted to speak to him alone."

"Who was the visitor?"

"We don't know, sir. He was dressed like a beggar in rags and kept his face covered. We assumed that Lanao was doing some private work with a spy for you or Emperor Daga. They were only alone for a couple of minutes. Sholl was stabbed in the chest and his throat was slit. Whoever this person was, he had been here before as he took Sholl's keys. There were probably fifty keys on that ring, and he knew and used the proper ones for both the doorway and the gate before he fled."

Commander Ichvain was pacing the room. "Bertrane!" he snapped "I should kick you in the face, but I need your help. Perhaps I'll kick you later." He turned to his associate. "Go back to town and spread the alarm that a murder has happened. It's no sense trying to track him. It has been too long."

"Sir," interjected Bertrane, "it has crossed my mind that this could be something the Emperor himself has masterminded. I wonder if this has anything to do with those soldiers being found slain on the wharf three weeks ago."

Ichvain stopped and smiled at Bertrane. "See, that's why I need you. You're absolutely correct. However, until I know otherwise, I will treat it just as it appears. If it's the Emperor, then he may just want to see how we would react."

Ichvain's partner left, and Ichvain sat down across from Bertrane again. "Also, until further notice, I am taking control of the prison facilities." Bertrane released a slight groan. "Do you have a problem with that, guard?"

"No, sire. It's just that Lanao has recently given most of the prisoners more freedom. I believe he has been expecting Emperor Daga to begin some releases. It seems to be working out fine."

"Working out fine?" the commander shot back. "The emperor has lost one of his best men today. He was murdered because of the laxity around here. If discipline had been tighter there is no way an old beggar would have been left alone with an excellent soldier in the emperor's army and been overcome."

"Of course, you're right, sir. I merely expressed what Lanao had been doing and I do work for him."

Ichvain gave Bertrane a cold stare. "Correction guard, you are now working for me. I thought I made that clear."

"Yes, sir! Of course, sir." He stood up and saluted him.

"Good. First order of business. Ensure all prisoners are secured."

Bertrane breathed a sigh of relief as he had sent all the prisoners back to their cells as soon as the murder had been discovered. "Sir, they are all in their cells."

"Of course they are in their cells, you idiot. That's where they belong. I want them in irons. The last thing I need now is some sort of a prison riot."

"I see," he said as his shoulders sagged.

"What?" he shouted.

Bertrane snapped to attention. "It will be exactly as you wish, sir. I'll see to it myself."

"Excellent. Then go away as I have some thinking to do."

The orders were received with some grumbling, not by the prisoners who had expected it sooner or later, but by the guards who had begun to enjoy the new working environment. When Bertrane returned, Ichvain was sitting back in Lanao's chair smoking one of the warden's cigars.

"Yes, what is it?"

"Your order has been filled, sir," he said with a salute.

"Of course, it has. Guard, if you have a job, go do it. You don't have to come back here every time you do something you've been told to do. When I give you an order, it will be completed. Is that quite clear?"

"Yes, sir!" he said as he turned and walked away.

"Oh, guard. One more thing," he said as he exhaled a huge cloud of smoke.

"Yes sir!" he said, turning back.

"Those two foreigners that were captured a few weeks ago, are they still here?"

"They are secure in their cells, sir."

"Bring them to me. I've heard a lot of nonsense about them and would like to speak with them."

A few minutes later, Mashua and Idiptu were escorted into the office and secured to two chairs which had been specifically designed for such meetings. Ichvain continued to smoke his cigar.

"Do you know who I am?" he asked as he stood up and began to pace about.

"Yes, sir," said Idiptu, "I was told you were some sort of local commander or something."

Ichvain coughed on his smoke. "Prisoner, is that supposed to be a title or what? Yes, I am some sort of local commander. However, I have another title. As Supreme Commander over the island of Leetra I am authorized to assume control over every aspect of life on this island. That includes assuming other duties during times of civil disobedience. I have assumed the title of Prison Magistrate." Idiptu and Mashua glanced at each other. "I have total authority over you and even over your lives. Do you know what that means?" He held up his hand to snap his fingers.

"Uh, excuse me, sir," said Mashua. Ichvain scowled at the interruption. "You may have assumed control over us, and you may even be able to have us put to death. However, no man has total authority over us."

Ichvain put his hand down and chuckled. "If I can kill you and I can obviously lock you up, how much more authority do I need?"

"You do not have any authority at all over our souls," said Idiptu.

"Your souls? Who on earth cares about your souls? However," he said as he sat down and snuffed out his cigar, "I did not call you in here so I could impress you with my power and attempt to frighten you."

"We're not frightened, sir," said Mashua, "so I am glad that was not your plan. However, can I ask you a question?"

Ichvain scowled at the snub and nodded. "Why are you so afraid of us?"

Ichvain laughed again. "I'm glad I called you in here. This is very entertaining. I am not the least afraid of any of these motley prisoners, least of all yourselves."

"A man does not have to shackle another man and lock him away if he is comfortable with him. Now, in the case of true villains who cannot be trusted by any, this is understandable. However, we have done nothing wrong, at all. We tried to do good to others. That's our crime."

"Well," Ichvain said as he slid nervously back in his seat. "Actually, these days, anyone going about doing good is immediately suspicious. Besides, the Emperor can have anyone jailed as he wishes."

"But the Emperor," Mashua continued, "has never reviewed our case. We were arrested because some man over on Afeena was being cruel to young women. Is that the nature of our crime?"

"The man you refer to is a Village Commander. He has total authority over those women, and if you were interrupting, then he had every right to arrest you."

"Did you hear him, Mashua?" laughed Idiptu. "He still thinks they have total authority."

"I should have you both beaten!" he yelled. "If you continue to be so impudent, I'll have you returned to your cell."

"That's fine, sir," said Mashua, "except for the smoke, we'd rather be here."

Ichvain released an exasperated puff of air. "I still have some questions. I understand that you can heal people."

"No, sir. Neither of us have any medical knowledge," said Idiptu.

"I don't think it was a medical thing but some sort of magic."

"Wrong again," said Mashua. "We aren't magicians, either."

"Then you had nothing to do with a group of men being healed? One man, they say, was blind."

"The sons of Lanao, Climus and Acton, brought some men who had been much burdened by Satan and asked us for help. We merely did what the Lord told us to do," said Mashua.

"So, some god or something caused them to be healed?"

"The Lord God Almighty," said Mashua, "who alone can heal and make right did these things. He will also judge the souls of men for their deeds at the end of time."

Ichvain sank back in his chair and was quiet for a minute as he thought. Finally, he spoke up. "I saw some of those men. I know they were in much better shape than before. But, what's this end of time thing?"

"There will be an end of time," said Idiptu. "What we know of life will be over. God will judge every person who has lived. Those who have done good and called out to the Lord God will be judged worthy and brought into God's perfect kingdom. Those who are evil, giving no care for God or seeking his will, shall be judged as well and sent to an eternal death in flames of fire."

"How do you know this?"

"Because God himself has revealed this to us and his people," said Mashua.

"Hmmp. Well, he won't be judging me because I don't believe in this superstition."

"The same God," said Idiptu, "that took those two dozen men and healed them will be judging you for what you have done. You must believe what you can see."

"Well, yes," he said as he lit another cigar and immediately put it out. "I know the men I saw were no longer ill from what they had before. If the effects are only temporary, I don't know. But it is a great gap between seeing a man get better and believing in the end of time and being judged to burn."

"Sir," said Mashua, "don't belittle what you know. Those men were cured of blindness and incurable skin diseases. They did not just get better. The God who can do these things will certainly judge both you and me."

"Well," he said, "it's interesting and I'm glad for those men who now feel better." Mashua buried his face in one hand. "However, I am not ready to join your beliefs. I just will not believe what I cannot see. Perhaps if you could show me something to convince me."

"Sir," said Mashua, "you have seen these men healed for no other reason. You will not believe me that a judgement will come until you are standing in front of God. Then, it will be too late. It is all a matter of faith. I cannot convince you to believe in God. You must simply choose."

"Perhaps you are right. So, I guess we are wasting our time. Guard!" Bertrane opened the door and stepped in. "We've had a nice talk, but it's time to return them to their cell."

"Yes, sir!" He unshackled them from the chairs.

"Oh, and guard."

"Yes, sir," he said, standing at a loose attention.

"Place them back in their cell, but there is no need to shackle them. I don't think they'll be going anywhere."

Bertrane stifled a smile. "Yes, sir." He led them out of the room.

Chapter 20

It was nearly noon when the Rasomites, along with John Dunley, deserted their boat near the north shore of Akadon. Though John had patched it as best he could, it still had sprung several leaks. An attempt was made to fix the leaks as they traveled. However, there was not a strong wind, so a great deal of rowing was involved. Therefore, whenever one of them stopped to repair a problem, their travel was slowed. It was a constant battle with the sea as they attempted to reach Akadon before the boat actually sank. Eventually, they were able to reach shore but could not drag the waterlogged boat to the beach. So, it was abandoned in shallow water.

They landed at the far end of Akadon from Getz, the capitol city. John figured it would be a twenty-mile trek to reach their destination, and they also would need to contend with a ridge of mountains which ran along the length of the island.

"However," John explained, "there are people on the island who will help us. There is a village nearby named Samta. Those people helped us a great deal during our final conflict with Coracus. It is unfortunate that my entire crew was lost in my last great battle."

"How can we be sure," Zoana asked, "that Samta has not met the same fate as the Farragon?"

"How far is Samta from here?" asked Anam. They were still on the beach near where they had come ashore.

John explained that it was less than two miles to the village. However, the trip there included a great deal of climbing.

"I think we are all ready to climb," Anam answered. "Do you feel up to it?"

"I feel better than I have in two years. I think I could even make the trip to Getz, but I'd like to find my friends first."

There was climbing, but it was much easier than the Rasomites had expected. In only a few minutes they came to an end of a mountain pass that overlooked what had been Samta. Samta had been a little mining village of about forty small wooden huts. It had been burned to the ground.

"It is as I feared," John said as he choked back tears. "I wanted to come up on this peak so I could see the village unaware."

Anam took his hand. "This will be hard, but I think we should go down there."

"Yes," John said. "Yes, I want to. Perhaps we can get a hint of what to do next."

"Perhaps you will grow so saddened," Paluqua warned him, "that you will lose your will to go on."

"However, I may," he said, "grow so angry as to go straight to Getz and kill that monster."

"Throwing yourself on the funeral fire," said Anam, "is not what is now needed. We need to be logical and we need to get direction from God. Let us do this. You and Crazon go into Samta. We shall stay right here and watch and pray. If you find nothing, then come back. If you do not return, we shall join you."

After some discussion, it was decided that Zoana would go with them and Anam and Paluqua would remain on the trail that overlooked the village. In a few minutes they could see the other three waving at them from below before they entered a partially burned house.

"Everything has been stripped," John commented the moment they entered. "You see, the people of Samta were extremely wealthy people. However, you wouldn't know it to see the outside of their homes. They worked the silver mines and kept most of the silver for themselves."

"But why would Coracus allow that?," Crazon asked.

"Because no one else dared enter the mines. The tunnels rose and fell dangerously. Also, many felt the mines were haunted. Coracus could never get anyone else to enter the mines. I guess, he finally didn't care."

"Where are the mines?" Zoana asked.

"Right underneath us," he laughed. "It's like a giant ant colony at our feet. The people made all sorts of ornaments and decorated their walls. Their stuff was really beautiful. Coracus must have stripped everything for himself."

They left that home and entered another one that still stood a few buildings away. John recoiled and stepped back as soon as they had entered.

"What is it, John?" Crazon asked him as he reeled about.

"Bodies…" he gasped.

Crazon entered and discovered the floor of the home was strewn with human bones that wild animals had cast about. She couldn't tell for certain, but there appeared to be the remains of four adults. This house, too, had been stripped of everything valuable.

"I'm sorry," she said as she came out. "I was afraid we would find something like this. What do you want to do?"

"I want to go on."

There were only six homes that were still partially standing, and they entered all six. All had been stripped clean. They found what they thought to be a total of fifteen bodies.

As they prepared to leave the last house, Zoana's alert sense of hearing detected people walking around outside. She motioned for the others to wait and looked through a crack in the wall. As she suspected, she saw a soldier, spear in hand, crouching behind a pile of burned timber.

"What should we do?" Crazon whispered.

"Well, you can be certain they're not going anywhere," she said. She crawled around the room, glancing out of every possible hole in an attempt to determine their number. "I don't know," she said with resignation. "I see at least three, but there could be many more concealed. What do you two think we should do?"

"I think we should go out fighting," John stated firmly.

"John," Crazon said, placing a restraining hand on his shoulder. "If we go out swinging at every opportunity, we shall never make it to Getz."

"Well," said Zoana, "we could go to Getz as prisoners."

"No!" snapped John. "I will never be a prisoner of that demon again. I shall die first. I say we fight it out."

"John," Crazon said calmly as she pointed at Zoana's knife belt. "There could be a dozen heavily-armed men out there. We have one knife between us. What sort of battle would that be?"

He snapped his gaze back and forth between them. "On Dernay, I heard so much of your great exploits for God. I don't believe they were just fables for children. What do you usually do about now?"

"Let's pray," said Zoana as she took the others' hands. "Almighty God, we put all of this into your hands. You are in charge here, Lord."

Suddenly, the entire building began to shake as the soldiers began kicking in the walls with their heavy boots.

"Here, let me help!" John yelled as he flew through the air, feet first against the wall. Crashing through the thin walls onto a surprised soldier, he knocked the man flat on his back. John, still on his feet, prepared to stomp the startled soldier, but was suddenly overcome by the rest of the attackers.

In a moment, his hands had been tied behind him and he'd been forced against the wall of the building.

"Who are you?" demanded the man who was obviously in charge. He prepared to slap John with his hand.

"I am your worst nightmare. What's the matter?" John sputtered. "Maybe I'm your grandmother, you son of a pig. What do you care?"

The captain, still poised to backhand him, suddenly punched John square in the jaw and knocked him cold. By now, Zoana and Crazon were being led from the house at the point of a sword. They glanced around and counted eight men.

"You've made a real big mistake," said Zoana to the captain. "When he wakes up, he's going to be even madder."

"Shut up!" he yelled. "Who are you people and what are you doing here?"

She looked at Crazon. "I'm confused. Does he want me to shut up or answer his questions?"

"I don't know, sister," Crazon answered. "Do you think we can take this bunch?"

"I'm not sure," Zoana answered as one of them engaged in tying her wrists behind her. "There's two of us and only eight of them."

Before he could secure the rope, she surprised him by grabbing both his wrists and stunned him by jerking him forward, slamming his face into the back of her head. Then she spun around and gave him a swift kick in the chest, sending him groaning to the ground. Another soldier rushed at her with a sword and confidently drew back for a swing. Zoana kicked his sword arm, breaking it and forcing him to drop his weapon. A third man rushed her with a lance. She somersaulted to the ground, startling him, and then leapt at his lance as he stood in an awkward position, breaking the shaft into splinters.

While Zoana was engaged, Crazon jumped into the air, causing the soldier who was trying to secure her wrists to lose his grip. She came down, wrapped her arm around his neck and jerked upward, nearly snapping his neck from his spine. The captain approached her with his sword drawn. She tried to kick his sword arm as Zoana had done but missed and tumbled to the ground. He drew his sword back to swing, but she heaved a handful of sand into his face and he fell back. She was on her feet when he came at her again. He swung at her and missed when she dodged. As he prepared to swing again, she took her instant of opportunity and punched him, cracking the bridge of his nose.

"I never did like bullies!" she yelled as he rocked back and forth, clutching his hand over his face. "That's what my friend felt like."

Zoana was now standing over her last attacker, holding the point of his broken lance to his face. She stepped back and waved the lance around. "Come on!" she yelled at the others as they backed off. "Who's next? We're just a couple of women. You ought to be more experienced at beating up women."

Crazon had gone to John as he was coming around, untied his wrists, and helped him up. He held one hand over his dislocated jaw and looked around at the injured. "How long was I out?" he mumbled as he took in the scene.

"Oh, only for a moment," she said. "Are you all right?"

He tried to open and close his mouth, which he did with some difficulty. "I guess I'll be fine. I'm glad I'm on your side."

"Now maybe you need to do some explaining," Zoana told their captain. "Why did you attack us?"

Still holding his hand over his cracked and bleeding nose, he answered her. "We are supposed to keep watch over this village and arrest trespassers." He wiped some blood from his face and stood erect in an attempt to look more dignified. "I still need to know who you are and what you are doing here."

Zoana nodded her head and took a deep breath. "That's a problem you'll keep for a while. I haven't really gotten my question answered yet. Why did you attack us? You could have asked us who we were without trying to knock the building down and tying us up." She nodded at John. "And hitting him when he couldn't protect himself was cowardly."

"No one can defy the Emperor's guard!" he snapped back.

"Oh, I see." She looked around again at the men bruised from battle. "So, what do you two want to do now?" she addressed her friends.

"We still need to reach Getz?" John said.

"If you could supply us with some horses," Zoana told the captain innocently, "we'd go away and leave you and your guarding alone."

He nervously rapped one hand against the other. "If you can find a horse on this side of the mountains, I'd be surprised. The emperor controls all the transportation. I just have one question. I've never seen anyone with flesh that shade. Where are you from?"

"Far away," Zoana told him. "You see, we're not telling you anything at all. If you can't help us reach Getz, we have no further use for you. So, you're free to go."

"Well," said John, ignoring the soldiers as well, "it's getting too late to head out today. I say we spend the night in one of the empty houses and leave in the morning."

"I agree," said Crazon.

"Well, there's one more thing," said Zoana. She looked back at the captain. "Do you have a shovel?" He told her he did. "Good. I need some of your men to bury these bodies. What has happened here is a sin against God and these people."

He backed off. "We're not burying these traitors. They got what they deserved. We still outnumber you and though we may get roughed up in a fight, we're not your servants."

"Do you have someone in command after you?" she snapped.

"I would take charge," said one of the other soldiers.

Zoana raised the broken lance which she still held. The captain, realizing he was defenseless, took another step back.

"Fine," she said. "After I plant this point into your captain's forehead you can get the shovel. Now, are you going to start digging or do we need to finish this fight?"

The captain looked angry but realized there was little he could do about it. "Someone go get the shovels."

Chapter 21

Mashua and Idiptu were awakened by the clink of a key in their cell door. Bertrane entered carrying a lantern. He held the lantern high in the air. "Commander Ichvain wants to see you again," he announced.

"Bertrane, what time is it?" Idiptu asked.

"I'm not sure. He woke me up as well. It is the middle of the night."

They were escorted back to Lanao's office where Ichvain was waiting. From the presence of the empty bottle on the desk and Ichvain's weary face, he'd obviously been up all night drinking.

They were seated in the prisoner's chairs and Bertrane prepared to secure them. Ichvain was leaning over the desk and appeared to be nearly asleep, but he shook his head and mumbled, "That won't be necessary." He waved Bertrane away.

Ichvain sat up in the chair. "Umm," he attempted to speak, but then sat silent with his eyes still closed. He finally shook his head violently as he tried to become more alert. "I've been thinking about our talk earlier. You are absolutely correct."

"Then," said Mashua as he leaned forward and placed his hands on the edge of the desk. "You are prepared to accept God as your Lord?"

"No. No. No," he said, shaking his head. "Not that. I mean, I think the emperor should review your case. I am sending you to Akadon on a boat this morning. Do you have any questions? First, let me say that I believe something is about to happen that I have waited for years to see."

Chapter 22

Marcis sat alone in Roda's house. The mother and daughter had gone into Laytruce to buy supplies. This was the first time since he'd arrived that he had been all alone. Of course, the women had gone outside often to tend to the garden and animals. Marcis had even gone out with them a few times the last couple of days. He felt he was strong enough to make the trip into town, but they all felt it would not be a good idea to take a stranger.

So, he sat and thought. For the first time since arriving, he truly missed his friends. Marcis was younger than any of the others and was not very interested in spiritual things. Rather, he'd always struggled through on his own or leaned upon the others. Now, supposing everyone thought he was dead and had therefore abandoned him, loneliness crept in. He had just decided to go out and groom the goats to take his mind off his problems when he heard the animals begin to sound the alarm that someone was coming. He quickly arose and glanced out the window to see two men in the distance. There had been no visitors since his arrival, and he was not certain how to act or whom he could trust. He decided to lay low rather than risk being discovered.

There came a rap at the door. "Roda! Shelley! We have good news."

"I told you they're not here, Acton."

"Roda! Is everything fine?" He waited. "I think we should go in and wait," he said more quietly. Climus pushed open the door and glanced around.

"Well?"

"There's no one home," Climus said. "But I think we should wait a bit."

"If they've gone into town, they could be gone all day. Even overnight. But we can wait a while."

He left the door ajar and they both sat on the steps in silence for quite a while. Marcis hid himself behind a bed but was in a position where his still injured chest was hurting real bad.

"Do you think she'll go with us" Acton finally asked.

"I told you she would, or I wouldn't have come."

"If they went into Laytruce for supplies, we might be able to find them there. It is market day."

"That's true," said Climus. "But if they're off in the hills picking berries or something, our trip will have been wasted."

They sat quietly for a while longer. Marcis had quietly moved and hidden himself behind a cabinet near the door so he could hear their conversation better. Due to his incompletely healed injuries, his position was no more comfortable than it had been near the bed. He gritted his teeth in pain and wished they would go away so he could find a more comfortable position. He knew that if he moved now, they would certainly hear him.

"I think we should go back to Laytruce," Acton finally said. "I'm almost certain they'd be in town."

"Why don't you go check there and I'll wait a little longer? I wouldn't want her to lose this chance."

"Climus, you know we have work to do for Moto."

"I know. I know. But I don't think we have anything more important to do than bringing Roda to see those men of God."

As soon as he heard that, Marcis nearly flew out of his hiding place and stumbled quickly to the door. The brothers leaped to their feet in terror until they realized it was just one man with a chest wrapped about with bandages and carrying a walking stick.

"Who are you?" Climus nervously asked.

"Never mind me. You said something about men of God. I must know everything."

"But who are you?" Acton countered.

Marcis, unable to support his weight any longer on his injured legs, slid onto the porch steps and sat. "My name is Marcis. I was left for dead by my comrades, but this good woman, Roda, and her daughter have doctored me up. Who are these men you speak of?"

"They are prisoners in the prison at Laytruce," said Climus. "Our father is the magistrate of the prison and treats them well. We were amazed when they healed our mother through the power of God, and so we brought our friends whom they also healed. I think if we took you, they could even heal you. We had hoped to take Roda to see them and see what could be done about her skin condition. They healed some men with the same condition."

"She's a good woman." Marcis smiled. "Despite her appearance, on the inside, she is beautiful."

"Yes, she is," said Acton. "That's why we thought of her. Many times, when we were young boys, she and her husband would bring us enough food to survive. Then, our father took over the prison and her husband died. We have always wanted to repay the favor."

"Well, it is as one of you said earlier, Roda and Shelley are in Laytruce and will be there for some time. But tell me of these men. Who are they?"

They looked at each other attempting to remember their names.

"Are they white men?"

"Yes," said Climus. "What else would they be? One is a large, muscular man."

"Ah, Mashua. It must be."

"Yes, Mashua," said Climus. "The other is Idiptu."

"Mashua, strong as a tree," mused Marcis. "Idiptu, gentle as a child and so smart. I would love to see them. I was thinking of them when you arrived."

"Then, let us all return to Laytruce.," said Acton. "We'll find Roda and Shelley at the market and then go to the prison."

"Go to the prison?" Marcis laughed. "I am afraid if I go there, it won't be as a visitor."

"Well," said Climus, "our father runs the prison. I am sure we can arrange something."

"Besides," said Acton, "no one will question us if we are seen walking around with an injured man. It has become normal activity for us lately."

Bertrane was sitting with Climus and Acton in the outer lobby of the prison as another guard stood by.

"I'm sorry, men," he explained, "but Commander Ichvain has assumed control of the prison. He sent the two from Ifintim to Akadon very early this morning. Your father left yesterday for a meeting with the Emperor."

"So that's where he disappeared to," said Climus as he remembered the messenger at the house the day previous. "However, is there any expectation of their return?"

"I have no idea. The Commander is calling all the moves now. He tells me very little. However, I'm sure their future lies more in the hands of the Emperor now than with anyone else. I would like to be of more help, but I really need to get back to my station now,"

"Yes, of course," said Acton. "Don't worry about us but send us a message when they return if you would."

"Yes, of course."

When they were back outside, they explained to Roda and Marcis what had happened. Shelley had remained at the market to finish shopping. They had not explained to Roda who these men were except that they were two men they really wanted her to meet. Marcis was deflated.

"Is there no way to Akadon?" he asked.

"Well," said Acton, "the Island Commander is in the prison. He's the only one who can get you off the island."

"Is he a reasonable man?"

"He's one of the Emperor's right-hand men. They are not to be trusted at all," said Acton. "But please don't tell anyone I told you that." Marcis caught him winking at Climus but did not understand.

"But if I want to reach Akadon, he's the only way through?" Climus added.

"That's correct," said Acton. "However, I think your wiser decision would be to go back to Roda's house and continue to wait as you get better."

Marcis stood quietly for a moment as he thought about his situation. "No," he finally said, "I just can't believe that you both happened to come out to the house. This must be God's plan."

"Then," Climus asked him, "I wondered if you also followed their God."

"My faith is not strong, I'll admit," he said. "However, this cannot be just like it looks."

"Then, what do you plan to do?" Roda asked nervously. "You don't mean to say that you're going in there?"

"I see no other way, my friend." He gave her a hug. "I thank you for all you've done. If not for you, I would most certainly be dead now. I hope someday to repay the favor."

"You need to also remember that stranger who brought you to the house," she reminded him.

"I do. In fact, I would not be surprised if he were close by right now. I've got to go now before I lose my nerve. I will be back." With that, he turned and limped across the road. Grabbing hold of the gate, he shook it as hard as he could.

A guard appeared at the window above. "What's with the racket?" he called out. "State your business."

"I am here to turn myself in."

"If you think we are running some sort of vacation getaway here," Ichvain shouted at Marcis, "you are absolutely crazy!"

Marcis sat in the prisoner's chair, but he was not secured. Bertrane stood by the door trying to subdue the smile he had at the audacity of this stranger.

"What are you looking so smug about?" Ichvain shot at him.

"Nothing, sir! Nothing at all! It's just a little humorous that this injured man showed up at our door asking for a ticket to Akadon."

Those were Marcis' words. He wanted a ticket to Akadon so he could join his friends.

"Sir," pleaded Marcis, "I know my request is a little unusual, but I have been at a great loss ever since I arrived on your island. My comrades, I am certain, believe I am dead. My great desire is to rejoin them. I have committed no crime. Please, be generous."

Ichvain sat at the desk quietly for a moment. His face was still red and contorted with anger. "You may have committed no crime. However, you trespassed onto Leetra and never completed the proper visitor passes. You have been hiding out like a renegade for several days. You have been eating and drinking rations which could have fed a tax-paying citizen. I could execute you as a spy. No crime?"

"Please try to understand, sir. The first week I was here, I was unconscious. It has only been the last couple of days that I could actually get up and move about without great pain. The trip into Laytruce would not have been possible before. If there are forms to fill out and taxes to pay, though I have no money, I will do my best to fulfill all the requirements. Do you truly believe that if I felt I was guilty of some great wrong I would come to see you? I just want to go to Getz or even to have a message sent to my friends."

"Sir, may I say something?" Bertrane asked. Ichvain glanced at him. "Do you remember how much grain and other supplies used to come to us from Ifintim? I can remember as a young man seeing the ships unloading. Also, remember how this very city got its name? Laytruce was the very place where the original treaty was signed with Ifintim before we were incorporated with Akadon. Now, here you have an emissary from a country with whom we still have a binding treaty. I know not what things are like in Ifintim. I hear things are horrible with monsters, but I do know this man is from a place we have a treaty with. Suppose they have rebuilt and now have a great army? They could make terrible enemies. Suppose he is the only one left. A land of opportunity, perhaps. You have such a chance here, sir, to receive great honor."

Ichvain looked at Marcis. "Tell me about Ifintim."

"It's true we were overrun for eighteen years with the curse of a man-eating race of creatures called Onoshe. However, they are gone now. We are rebuilding our homeland. Though we are few, we are mighty. Sir, our only purpose for coming here was to seek peace again between our people. We did not know how we would be received, so first we sought to know what kind of people lived here."

"And," Ichvain asked as he stroked his chin, "what have you found out concerning the generosity of our people?"

"Thus far, the people have treated me as a guest and offered great kindness. I now sit here waiting to see what the official government action will be."

"I see. Bertrane," he said to the guard, "take this man away. That is, have him wait somewhere while I think this through. My mind is running counter to its own self. I need to think."

Chapter 23

A cool, damp wind blew between the planks of the dilapi-dated house Crazon, Zoana, and John Dunley had occupied. Still, it was better than sleeping in the open, especially with the soldiers constantly lurking about. John and Crazon had slept while Zoana had kept a watch. She had no great fear of the soldiers, but her confidence was aided even more with the knowledge that Anam and Paluqua were also out there watching everything. It was dark in the house, but the soldiers had struck campfires in the distance on both sides of the building. This assisted greatly for her to keep a better eye on them. She had figured out that there were about thirty men left guarding Samta. Why it was of such great importance to guard a burned-out village, she could not understand. Apparently, there had been other curiosity seekers in Samta, and the Emperor wanted to know what the great interest could be. So, he had added this great guard. The presence of these three intruders made their captain extremely nervous, but except to keep an eye on them, the soldiers did not want to hassle with them anymore. The three could not understand why they hadn't been detained and hauled off to Getz instead of being merely watched.

Zoana realized John was awake and watching her. "Sleep comes hard when you feel like a prisoner, doesn't it, John? Don't worry, Paluqua and Anam are watching them, I am sure."

"I am not worried at all, Zoana. But I have been wondering over their curious activity and something I overheard."

"What was it you heard?"

"While they were burying the dead, I was standing near the captain as he told two of the soldiers to ensure that all of the mine entrances were sealed off. I thought at first they were afraid we were trying to steal silver, but later I heard two other guards whispering, so I moved behind them. One of them said he was certain the traitors would make an appearance."

"What traitors?"

"Zoana, I think they believe the people of Samta will attempt to sneak back into the village. I don't understand. I just feel like something strange is about to happen."

"Then why the big fires?" she asked. "They ought to be lying low."

"Have you been impressed with their intelligence so far? I am sure they think we know what is going on. They are watching us to see what we'll do or if anyone tries to contact us. They're using us like bait, which is why we haven't been arrested. I also am sure they don't know where all the entrances are."

"So, what do you suggest?"

"I wish the three of us could get out of here. I know that no one is coming to us. I think we should go to them."

"Crazon and I could sneak out of here anytime. They cannot see us at night and our eyesight is ever so much better than theirs."

"I'm willing to try it. I've done enough of my own sneaking away from his troops myself." He tapped Crazon on the shoulder. "Hey, sleepy, we're heading out."

"What's going on?" she asked as she sat up, instantly alert.

John reviewed everything he had told Zoana.

"Well, I heard something else," Crazon said. "They are afraid to go near the mines because they think it's haunted."

"With so much death around here," said Zoana, "it very well may be."

They silently climbed out of the house in a space between two loose planks, since they knew the door was watched, and passed a guard to freedom. When they were some distance away, John told them of one secret entrance to the mine the soldiers were almost certainly unaware of. However, it was very close to one of the fires the soldiers had built.

When they were almost within the light of the fire, they froze in place when one of the soldiers called out to stop. Strangely enough, all five of the men who were gathered around the fire grabbed their weapons and ran off in the opposite direction. They lay quietly in the dark for a few seconds to ensure that it was not a trap.

Zoana was surprised when a voice out of the darkness whispered to hush and follow him. She could make out the shape of a person all shrouded in black and told the others to follow her. Only a few feet away, they heard the dull thunk of a wooden door closing. Now, it was even darker than it had been above. However, Zoana and Crazon moved confidently along, keeping their partner between them as they followed the darkened form. Then, they heard what sounded like a metal door close. They could see a small shaft of light coming from a few paces away.

A door opened where the shaft of light had been coming through a small window at its top and the room filled with light as two heavily shrouded men entered with lanterns. A third figure, also wearing dark clothing with his face streaked with black, sat on the floor nearby. He was the one they had followed.

The room they now were in was obviously a part of the mine. However, there was no silver present now, only bare stone walls. Behind them was a large metal doorway through which they had entered. Beyond them, through the other doorway, was another little room through which the other two had entered. This appeared to be an office. The three suddenly realized they were still on their hands and knees since they had crawled in, and the two men were standing over them. Standing up and dusting themselves off, Zoana, who was still in the lead, extended a hand to the two men.

"I think I need to thank you," she said to them.

There was no way to identify either of the men with their dark clothing, hoods, and their faces streaked black with soot. The one standing in front raised his palms, indicating he was not ready for that formality yet.

"Who are you?" he asked.

"I'll tell you this," John offered. "We're no friends of Coracus."

"That does not concern us since Coracus is dead."

"Coracus is dead?" John exulted. "Then everything has changed!"

"No, I'm afraid not. Very little has changed as his chamberlain, Daga, is now in charge. I can tell these two women are not from here. However, I envy their...uh..." He waved his hand up and down as he gazed at their dark skin. "But you seem somehow familiar," he said to John.

"I've been here before," he said, "but I'd rather not reveal my name just yet."

"Because everyone believes you to be dead. Is that right, John?" said the other man. He looked at his partner. "It's John Dunley, sir."

"Oh, my word, so it is," he said. He extended a hand. "Welcome home, John. Perhaps everything has indeed changed if the dead are returning to help us."

"Thank you," he said as he shook hands. "I have been on an extended vacation nearby. You know I won't truly be home until I reach Afeena."

The man shook his head. "I know that, my friend, but you'll always have a home here."

"To whom am I to be so indebted?"

"Oh, I'm sorry," he said, laughing. He wiped some of the soot from his face.

"Moto!" John said, shaking his hand exuberantly. The other men identified themselves as well, and they all exchanged hugs.

"Moto was one of our greatest helpers during Afeena's battle for independence." John explained to the women. "Of course, our mutual goal was that we both be free from the demon-possessed emperor and restore order on all three islands. I guess it was just not meant to be at that time."

"However, the time is ripe," said Moto. "We are very organized in our preparation for the battle for freedom now. Daga's troops are weary and inefficient. We have spies throughout the army. With Coracus' death, we shall take advantage of the confusion." He addressed the women. "We have seen you in battle. We would be pleased if you would join us. This is why we brought you here. We have betrayed ourselves into your hands. So, if you will not join us, we do not know what to do with you. Please, join us."

"Crazon," said Zoana. "Let's discuss this." They went into a corner and quietly conferred.

"But," said John to Moto as the women planned. "I thought you were all dead. The silver is gone. The village is burned to the ground. There are soldiers standing guard."

"Alas," Moto said, gazing downward, "our people have been all but destroyed. When the village was raided two years ago, nearly everyone was slaughtered. A handful went to slave work in the quarries. Most of the rest were routinely executed whenever Coracus felt the whim. There are only a few dozen of us here. But in his stupid desire for total control, he has murdered his allies as quickly as his enemies. Everyone hates him."

"Moto, the people of my home. How do they fare?"

"Conditions on Afeena are worse than on either Akadon or Leetra. All of the men and boys on Afeena were removed from the island and placed into forced labor. Most are now dead. The young women and older girls were either sent here or a few went to Leetra as house servants. Things on Afeena are sad and quiet as all that remains are women and a few little children, as well as a light guard. Do you know that no one even knows how many are left in the Isles? When I was a boy and all the islands were at peace and governed separately, there may have been as many as fifteen or twenty thousand people. Now, because of the murder and disease, there may be half that or less. This insanity has got to stop."

"You said you had spies throughout the Isles. Are they people of power?"

"One of our greatest helpers has hardly played his hand as of yet. If he has the nerve to join us now, and with your help to represent Afeena, we could quickly gain the upper hand."

"But my curiosity rages. Who is this man you speak of?"

"First, I must know," said Moto. "Do you intend to join us?"

"My angry spirit wants revenge. The man inside my flesh wants to move out now. However," he glanced at the women, "I have sworn allegiance to my rescuers and those who taught me about God."

"God?"

"Yes," he nodded, "John Dunley now belongs to the Lord Almighty."

"Then it truly is a miracle. Two of our greatest spies on Leetra have also been telling everyone about the Lord. In fact, people have been healed of the plague. Even the prison magistrate on Leetra is one of them and has befriended two of these people. But we know nothing of God. Please tell us everything. This very God could be the force which will truly unite us in our cause against evil."

The women had been listening to the conversation and had stopped conferring when Moto spoke of his desire for God.

"Do you really want to know about my Lord?" Crazon asked him.

"Yes. Yes, we all do."

"Then, that should be the first order of business."

"But wait," Zoana interjected. "What can you tell me of these two on Leetra?"

"I am sorry," said Moto. "News travels so slowly between the islands. Everything is done in whispers. All I know is that the prison magistrate there has befriended them, and they are well cared for. "Come with me." Moto went into the office area with his two men and the others followed.

Beyond the office they went through another huge metal doorway and entered the mine itself. The walls glistened in the lamplight with the presence of precious metal. A few paces along the fairly narrow passageway they entered a cavern. They were in the presence of about thirty men, most of whom were similarly dressed in black as the other three.

"Everyone come here quickly!" called out Moto. "These women can teach us about the same God the people of Leetra have been hearing about." He looked back at Zoana. "However, I have neglected to ask you, do you intend to join us?"

"First," Crazon told him as she placed her hand on his shoulder, "let us tell you about ourselves and about God. Then, we shall talk of alliances."

"Of course," he said quietly, sitting on the floor as the rest of the men gathered around him. "Please, tell us everything."

So Zoana and Crazon told them everything. They told them how their people had been nearly destroyed by the Atrocenes, but how in the end, God had vindicated them. They told them of the evil priests in Foramen and how, in a moment, they were all destroyed. They told them how God had created an oasis in the desert. They told them of the hopeless war that never happened between Lasapulis and Chiam and how these people found God and became friends. They told them how a handful of ragtag migrants in the desert completely destroyed a savage army. They told them how they had arrived in the valley of Ifintim and how Mashua's people had lived for eighteen years in a cave for fear of the dreadful Onoshe and how they were delivered in one night. They finally told them why they had come to the Isles, that is, to lead them all to God and to create a peace better than before.

John excitedly filled in the blanks from the stories they had told him while on Dernay.

"So, you see," Zoana finished, by now it was nearly dawn, "if all you do is organize yourselves to go out and do violence to the violent, you are edifying their evil. I certainly do not advocate going to them in peace. They have proved themselves not to be trusted."

"Then what are we to do?" called out one of the men. "Are we to live in this cave in fear like your man, Mashua, and his people did? Where can we go to find peace and live our own lives?"

"You must go to God and offer him your life," Crazon told him. "It was never yours to begin with. You didn't create it and it's not yours to take away."

He stood up and approached Crazon. There were tears streaking across his blackened face. "My wife is dead. I do not know where my children are. My village is burned. My leaders have betrayed me." He shrugged his shoulders. "I have little else to lose but my life. So, I may as well give the one thing I have willfully, rather than waiting for that also to be snatched away from me."

Crazon hugged him. "I know your grief. I have been there." There were tears in her eyes, as well. "What is your name?"

"My name is Geen."

"Geen, please pray with me." And she led him in a sinner's prayer.

One by one, all of the men came forward and repeated similar prayers. As they did so, many of the sad and burdened faces started showing signs of joy. Eventually, they started to clap their hands. The women taught them a song, but the echo of the cavern made it reverberate into an ear-splitting din. Then Moto, remembering the soldiers camped outside almost directly above them, hurriedly sent a man to see what was happening. He returned a few minutes later, laughing.

When he had gotten everyone to settle down, he explained. "Here in the mine, it is very noisy, but outside, our wailing and singing sounds like a hundred giants. The soldiers, all of them, have deserted. I went out and walked about freely. They are gone from Samta. They even left some of their weapons." He held up a spear he had retrieved. He looked at the women, holding the spear in front of him with both hands. "This has proven to me that our unity and God is all that matters. This," he broke the spear over his knee, "is powerless. They may come back and take my life, but they cannot defeat me. The moment I die I will be in the arms of God."

Everyone began to shout and dance about. Moto cornered Zoana.

"This is the happiest day we have had since the day we thought our forces and those of Afeena could defeat Coracus, only to become disappointed. No, this is the greatest day of my life. You were wise in waiting to decide about joining forces with us because, now, I want to join forces with you."

Anam and Paluqua had watched all the activities of Samta from their perch over the village. They had seen the fight the day before but forced themselves not to interrupt. They had seen the little house surrounded, knowing at some point the three inside would escape into the night. They had even seen the shadowy figures moving through the darkness and surmised who they were and why the soldiers had a sudden interest in Samta. Then, in the early dawn, they had heard the frightening roar emanating from seemingly nowhere. They didn't interfere because they knew the Lord had planned the entire thing. They had seen the terrified soldiers running into each other and, finally, run away. Even their captain fled with them, apparently in the direction of Akadon.

"What should we do?" Paluqua asked Anam.

"I think we should follow them."

"But what about the others?"

"They'll know where we've gone. They'll be fine."

It was not difficult for them to follow the runaway soldiers. The men stayed on the road most of the time, and Paluqua and Anam followed them at a great distance. The clatter of the metal weapons and armor could be heard from nearly a mile away. The Rasomites were no longer afraid of being seen but were actually eager for some activity. The soldiers knew where all the watering spots were and stopped often. This allowed Anam and Paluqua to be privy to their conversations. There wasn't much to hear, as whenever the men stopped, there was little talking since they were so out of breath. The men had already believed there were demons of the dead living in Samta. Now they were convinced. However, the captain finally advised them to be consistent in their tale-bearing and announce that an army of several hundred had been raised to crush the empire.

Due to all their running, the soldiers took many breaks. It was late afternoon when they reached Getz. When they arrived in town, the captain hastily organized his men into proper military formation. Then, as he called cadence, they proceeded to march the last mile to the palace. Anam and Paluqua, now no longer concerned for being seen, followed them at a few hundred paces.

Naturally, these oddly colored, scantily clad newcomers drew a crowd. However, though they passed government officials and armed troops, no one interfered with them. The captain and his men had already passed through the outer palace gate when the Rasomites arrived. There were a number of palace guards on duty, and their entrance was barred.

"Where do you think you are going, stranger?" a guard snapped at them. He looked the two Rasomites up and down,

put off by Anam's hulking size, but pleased by Paluqua's figure and dress.

Anam pointed toward the entrance and said nonchalant-
ly, "We need to go inside and tell your emperor what happened out at Samta this morning."

"What do you know about Samta?"

"We were out there yesterday when your forces came under attack." Paluqua stifled a smile as he continued. "They
were doing their duty and attempted to take three prisoners
who were prowling about the village. Your men were beaten
off and the prisoners escaped."

"Do you know where the escapees are now?"

"They disappeared during the night. Listen, I don't mean
to show any disrespect, but I would like to give our eyewit-
ness account to the emperor."

"The emperor is unavailable. However, I'll see what can
be done." He quickly dispatched a messenger to the captain
of the troop which had just been admitted. "Tell him," he
said out of the Rasomites' earshot, "that they claim to have
seen the battle. I don't know what's going on, but just get
that message to him before he is interviewed."

The messenger returned with two other palace guards a
few minutes later, apologizing to his captain. "I tried to inform him before he went into the conference room, but it was
too late. When the chamberlain found out there were other
witnesses, he said he wants to hear them as well."

The other two guards escorted Anam and Paluqua inside.
Before they were admitted, Anam had to relinquish his knife.
Paluqua had no weapon. The room they entered was a large
meeting room. Behind a huge wooden table sat Daga's chamberlain and two other men. The captain of the troops from
Samta was on his feet, speaking to the chamberlain. Four of
the captain's exhausted men were seated. There was also a

palace guard at each end of the table. When Anam and Paluqua entered, the chamberlain rose and stared at them in awe.

"I was told we had two very interesting visitors, but I didn't expect such strange looking savages."

"We are not savages, sir," said Paluqua. "We are people of God on assignment to the Isles of Aboti."

The captain interrupted. "Be careful, sir. These are of the same race of people who attacked us yesterday."

The chamberlain addressed Anam. "What is your mission?"

"To bring the peace of God to this place."

The chamberlain sat down and conferred with his two men, then looked back at Anam. "I'll be asking some questions to verify your truthfulness."

"Speak on, sir," Anam answered. "I'll answer as best I can."

"How many are you?"

"When we first arrived here there were eight of us."

"And their status?"

"I am not certain, sir. However, one we fear died upon our arrival to Leetra. Three more were lost on Afeena and, I believe, were taken in by your people. They may have been arrested. Two of us stayed behind in Samta this morning."

"How did you get here?"

"You mean to reach Getz, sir?" The chamberlain nodded. Anam pointed to the captain. "We followed him in, sir. He led us right to the palace."

"How could you allow something like that?" he snapped at the captain.

"We didn't know they were there, sir. They must have been under cover."

Anam shook his head. "No, sir. Most of the time we walked down the middle of the road directly behind your men."

"Could no one even look over his shoulder?" the chamberlain snarled. "Excuse me," he addressed Anam, "I never got yours or the woman's name."

"Anam."

"My name is Paluqua," she said. "I take offense at being called a savage. However, I will consider that you neither receive many visitors nor have much opportunity to leave. So, your experience is limited."

The chamberlain leapt to his feet. "This is an outrage having this person come in here and spew out insults."

"I have made no insults," she said. "I have stated facts." She glanced at Anam.

"Remember your God," he said. "Tell the man more than he wants to know."

"That man," she pointed at the captain, "has betrayed you! There are no massive armies in Samta. The attackers he referred to were the very prisoners he unsuccessfully tried to apprehend. Two women."

"Is this true?" the chamberlain asked the captain.

"Of course not. Many of my men were seriously injured when we were ambushed."

"Did you tell him how your nose was broken?" she asked him.

"I was engaged in battle with an enemy soldier."

She looked at the chamberlain. "My sister punched him in the face for a similar assault on a friend of ours who could not protect himself."

"I do not battle women!" the captain shouted.

"Of course, you don't, when you can more easily beat them senseless. You were beat up by a woman and then became her servant."

"I serve no woman!"

"Perhaps you would like to demonstrate your prowess against myself," she offered.

The captain stared at her silently.

"You seem to have lost your bravado and your temper, captain. Do you accept her challenge?" the chamberlain asked.

"I do not fight women," he snarled.

"Then challenge me," Anam offered. "I came here in peace, but sometimes a point must be made before a goal can be reached."

"That's enough!" snapped the chamberlain as he took his seat. "If there's to be any brawling, please do it elsewhere. You mentioned one word earlier that I wish to pursue."

"Was that word 'God', sir?" Anam asked.

"Exactly. Where did you sail from?"

"We sailed from Itintim." The chamberlain scratched his chin as he thought. "Are you considering our comrades, sir? I am very concerned for them."

"They are fine, though in bonds. Now tell about this God."

"I cannot tell you everything. I can tell you only through him can you find salvation. Only through him can you find lasting peace."

"These are the same words the others spoke. They seem innocent, but they also smell of revolution. These words are the reason the others are still in prison."

"You can bind them, and you can bind us, here and now, but you cannot bind our souls. We belong to God," Paluqua said.

"Yes, I know," he smiled. "These are the same words the others said. I am not concerned with your afterlife."

"Don't you understand what you are doing?" Anam asked him. "By opposing us, you are also opposing God. He does not make a good enemy."

"We have maintained this position for most of our lives," he answered. "We are doing fine, so far."

"Beware," Anam said. "Do not be like a man who leaps from a great cliff and before hitting the ground believes he is doing fine, so far."

"An interesting play on words."

"For a savage," Paluqua added.

The chamberlain stood up again. "Let's make something clear. This meeting, and the reason I brought you two in here, was to determine if there was any hostile activity in Samta. I believe you've offered your information and you are now free to leave,"

"We don't intend to leave without our comrades," Paluqua said.

"The three prisoners we have are going nowhere until the Emperor himself says so. If you don't leave now, you may lose your opportunity to do so."

"Consider our opportunity lost," said Anam. "We cannot leave."

"Guard!" the chamberlain called out. The guard at the door allowed two other guards to enter, and Anam and Paluqua were peaceably led away.

Chapter 24

Commander Estigan climbed down from his horse. He tied the reins to a post in front of his house and ran his hand along the animal's sleek coat. The horse had been given to him by Commander Borda as a gift. Estigan had coveted such a thing for the two years since he had been stuck in Mendoa. He felt the horse's soft muzzle. It was not a young, strong animal, but it still pleased him greatly. He could see himself patrolling the streets astride his new steed and making an emergency trip to Artuna to speak with his commander.

He glanced at his house and realized it was dark inside. The sun was just beginning to set, and he figured they ought to be lighting the lanterns, especially the outside lanterns, in expectation of his return. He had not wanted to come home as he expected more conflicts, but he had worn out his welcome finally and decided to return before Borda ordered him to return home. There had been a good time drinking and dining. They'd discussed the prisoners at great length. Ahohiel had been sent to Akadon on the morning boat after Commander Borda had interviewed him with little success. They had also talked about Estella. In the past he felt he had been too flexible and too forgiving. However, no more. He had determined to be as firm as a rock.

One of his men had finally noticed him from down the street and was approaching him. "It's about time!" he lashed out angrily, instantly changing from his more contemplative state of mind. "I am sure you must have heard the horse from quite a distance."

The guard laid a hand on the horse's back. "It's a fine-looking animal, sir. I'm sorry. We were all at the other side of town."

"And how can you guard the entire town if all of you are way over there? Never mind. Take the horse to the stable, give it the best oats and some hay and water. Clean out a stall and wipe her down real good."

"Sir, I don't believe there are any oats."

"Then, do your best. She is a gift from Commander Borda. You will be responsible for taking care of her."

"Yes, sir!" He untied the reins and led the horse away.

Estigan looked at his darkened house again. Except for the monotonous sound of a single chirping cricket, all was silent. Then, he heard the sound of far off voices. They seemed to be singing or chanting in unison. He wished he'd kept the horse to avoid the long walk, but he felt it would be good to stretch his legs after the long ride. Estigan headed for the other side of town as something gnawed at him that this was a new disturbance.

Walking the streets in the direction of the noise, he ground his teeth as he observed that every house was darkened. Only a few had the forethought to light the outside lantern. At first, when he heard the sound, it seemed to be many people singing together, but the closer he got the more it began to sound like nonsense. The voices were not in unison, nor were they even using words he had ever heard. It was actually causing his head to throb and the hair on the back of his neck to bristle.

When he reached the end of the street, he could see into a clearing just inside the woods. Approaching the clearing, but partially hidden by the trees, he was amazed at the number of people gathered. There must have been nearly two hundred women and several children. Huddled together in one area were seven of his eight guards; the only men present. The one guard absent was attending to Estigan's horse.

As he stood there, still suffering from their awful noise, one of his guards stood up and headed in his direction. Estigan glanced over his shoulder and realized they could see the front of his home a couple hundred yards back down the street. They had been looking out for him. He thought of bursting into their ridiculous gathering and waving his horse whip about to scatter them. He realized he'd left the whip with the horse. He backed behind a tree as the one guard came to within a pace of where he had been standing. The man looked steadfastly down the street toward Estigan's house and then glanced in both directions. Shrugging his shoulders, he turned about and was startled by the imposing presence of Commander Estigan.

"What is going on here?" he shouted over the din. "Who authorized this meeting?"

"No one authorized it, sir. It just sort of happened," the guard stuttered.

"If I had my whip, I'd beat your face bloody!" He waved his hands frantically over his head. "Now you get back in there and then, you and your pathetic sidekicks disburse this crowd."

"I…I can't do that, sir."

"Are you disobeying an order?"

"I don't want to disobey you, sir. It's just that I don't feel I have the right to disturb them."

"You don't feel you have the right? What are you blubbering about? What's going on here, anyway?"

"It's a miracle, sir. The entire town has come out and we are all seeking God's wisdom."

"Is that what this is? More of those lying foreigners' foolishness? I'll take charge."

He spun around and dashed into the crowd screaming at the top of his voice. "Everyone listen to me! This must end now, or harsh consequences shall follow!" A few that sat nearby became silent, but hardly anyone else could hear him as most still continued in their prayer and singing. He was prepared to kick one woman when Regina appeared from the crowd and approached him. She fell at his feet and wrapped her arms around his legs. This frustrated him as he had no idea how to react. For a moment he considered kicking her aside, but thinking better of it, he roughly grabbed hold of her shoulders and hoisted her to a standing position. Then, he realized she was crying her heart out.

"Oh, Daddy, I'm so sorry for the way I've acted. Please forgive me and let's start over."

Still angry, but subdued, he snapped at her. "Of course, I forgive you. Now what's going on here? This foolishness must stop."

"Oh, Daddy, I love you," she whined. "Please tell me you love me. Do you love me?"

"Of course, I do, dear. Now you have to get hold of your senses."

She was tenderly kissing him on the cheek. "Tell me you love me."

"I said I did! Now come on."

"But say it, please. I want to hear those beautiful words."

"Yes, I love you!" he yelled at the top of his voice, preparing to rebuke her again. He suddenly realized the entire assembly was sitting in silence, listening to and staring at him. His face turned crimson with embarrassment.

Regina continued to brush his cheek with her lips. "Oh, Daddy. Don't be ashamed. It's okay if you love your daughter."

His wife and his other daughter were now approaching him. His wife also had been crying.

"Daddy! Daddy!" Lora called out as she tore free from her mother and ran to him.

Reluctantly, he picked her up as he normally did.

"Guess what, Daddy. Everyone loves each other and we all love God. Isn't that good news. Aren't you glad? Isn't that good news, Daddy?"

"Yes, that's good news," he whispered to her.

She turned her head around and shouted out, "Daddy's glad, too! Now everyone's happy."

He put Lora down as his wife approached him. "What is going on here?" he snapped.

"It seems pretty obvious. The whole town is reaching out to God in unity. More than anything else, I want you to become part of this."

"Become part of this?" he snarled. "This is nonsense. This is something those foreigners have infected you with."

"Yes, they did begin it. They infected us with love. Is that a bad thing?"

"I could hear you all from the other side of town. It sounded like a meeting of crazy people. What was that noise you were making?"

"We were each reaching out to God Almighty in our prayer language that he gave us. We were striving for, and reaching, love and harmony. Won't you join us?"

"Who organized this thing?" His eyes fell upon Estella as she came from the crowd. "I should have known you'd be in the middle of this!" He raised his hand to strike her. Then, he had to shake his head to clear his mind because he thought he was hallucinating. He knew she had approached him with her empty hands raised toward him. He figured someone had passed her a sword. He couldn't understand how a little thing like she could wield such a huge weapon. It was one of the largest swords he had ever seen. He backed up two or three paces. "What do you intend to do?" he asked her as he nervously eyed the sword.

"I intend to love you, regardless of any evil you intend. But, please, I'd rather you'd join us." She took another step forward, and he realized the sword was gone. "What do you intend to do, Commander Estigan? It's time to choose your side."

He looked her in the eye and then up and down. She looked at once so sweet and innocent and, again, so terrifying and imposing as her eyes seemed to slice right into his soul. As he considered asking her again to explain herself, a seething hatred came upon him. Suddenly, without warning, his fist swung at her and struck her in the face almost exactly where he'd hit her the day before.

There was stunned silence, and even Estigan was surprised at his sudden burst of anger. Then he yelled out, "That's enough! Now everyone go home!" He pointed at his men. "If you fools do not immediately reestablish order here and continue your service, you will be harshly reprimanded. I am so angry now I may even ask for your execution. Make your first order of business to resecure your prisoner. She has caused enough trouble." The men were moving ever so slowly toward Estella as though they were uncertain how to act. One of them got down and attempted to revive her.

Estigan's wife approached him, and he raised his fist again. "Don't make me do this!" he yelled out.

Then he realized his own men had surrounded him. "What? What do you fools want now? I ordered you to restore order to this assembly."

"I'm sorry, sir," said one of the guards. "The only way of restoring order is to safeguard you."

He felt his hands being shackled behind his back. "What are you stupid fools doing?" He struggled to get free, but it was impossible. "You'll never get away with this outrage. I'll see to that. I demand you release me at once."

Once he was confined to the town prison in the same cell Estella had previously occupied, they unshackled him, and he attempted to leap upon one of the guards. However, the other man restrained him without violence until they were all safely out of the cell. He was still stunned when he heard both his cell door secured and then heard the outer gate, which they never locked, secured as well.

"I'll get out of here!" he screamed. "I'll wring all your necks. I'll see you all hung together." Though he continued his rantings, except for one guard who remained on duty, no one at all could hear him.

There were no medical facilities in Mendoa. The only thing close to filling such a need was the house used as guard quarters. The guards kept a supply of bandages and a few medicinals in the unlikely event they should get hurt on duty. It was here they carried the unconscious body of Estella. Some cold water and a whiff of some nasty smelling whiskey revived her, but she was still dizzy, and her head was throbbing again. She was in good spirits, however.

"Ahohiel never told me that working for God required face protection," she quipped as she sat on the edge of the dining room table which doubled as a medical bed.

"We have a couple of extra helmets," one of the men joked. "Would you like one?" He was smiling at her.

"I'll pass for now." She looked around. Four of the guards were present, as well as Regina.

"Mother took Lora home for bed," Regina said. "She figured she'd had enough excitement for one day."

"And everyone else?" Estella asked her.

She shrugged her shoulders. "I guess my father got his way and everyone went home."

"And your father?" She glanced at the guards.

"I'm afraid we had to lock him up for the night," one of them said.

"I feel sorry for him," she said. "I mean, he doesn't understand. I wish there was something I could do."

"If everything's fine then," Regina said, "I think I'll go home as well. Will you be okay?"

"I'm sure I will. You go ahead, Regina," she said as the girl departed. "Please pray for your father."

"Don't worry, Estella. He's at the top of my list."

After Regina left, one of the guards asked if she'd like to be escorted home.

She thought for a moment. "No, could you take me to wherever Commander Estigan is?"

"He's easy to find." One of the guards laughed. "He's in the same cell you were in."

A few minutes later, she and one of the guards reached the prison and opened the outer gate. It was dark outside now. There were two small torches, one over each of the outside and inside prison doors. There was also a lantern over the shack where the other guard had been posted.

"I don't think it would be a good thing for you to get too close to him," her escort warned.

"I understand. I just want to talk with him."

He escorted her down the stone steps but stayed out of sight as she approached the door. When she looked through the little window, he was staring blankly at the door in the darkened room. There was a small torch above the door, so she was clearly illuminated.

"I knew someone was here. I heard the gate," he said, "but I never expected you."

"I am sorry for how things have turned out for you. You seemed to have mellowed out some."

He gritted his teeth. "I'd still like to snap your neck. But I know having a fit in here won't help any. I'll be out soon, and then, I'll clean house. You'll be swinging from a rope in Artuna. No, maybe right in front of your house as a warning to any other trouble-makers."

"I don't know why you hate me so much."

"Because you want to destroy the whole order of things."

"This all began with just wanting my family back. Is that so hard to understand? If having families ripped apart is part of your order, then I guess you're right. I want to destroy that."

"I'll straighten you out when I get out of here. I'll have all of Mendoa swinging if that's what it takes."

"Why? Why all the senseless killing? It's so much nicer to love and help each other. But I didn't come here to argue about your beliefs. I came here to give you something much better. Estigan, submit yourself to God. Reach out to him. People are praying for you. Choose between eternal death and eternal life."

"When I get out of here, I won't even authorize a trial for you. My first action will be to see you hang."

"You really are something. I'd best be going, but I brought this for you." She passed a sack through the window in the door.

He walked over to inspect the contents of the sack. It contained half a baked chicken, a piece of cheese and some fruit. He looked at her speechless.

"I was afraid you may have missed dinner. It's something the guards put together."

"Why did you do this?" he asked quietly.

"Because whether you believe it or not, I love you with the love of God. God bless you, sir. Good night." She smiled at him and left the prison.

"Well," her escort asked her once outside in the dark and heading toward her house. "What's next?"

"I still hurt. I'm going home and get some sleep. Of course, I'll be praying before I pass out. I have no idea what tomorrow holds, but I certainly expect life to never be dull again."

"Oh, do you know what he said before we locked him up? I think it was the reason he backed off from you at first. He thought someone had given you a sword."

"Really?"

He nodded. "Yes, he swore you were holding one of the greatest swords he'd ever seen. His eyes must have been playing tricks. Well," he said as they reached her house, "here we are. You sleep well. If anything comes up during the night, you feel free to come over to the barracks. Of course, we'll be making our rounds and will keep an eye on you and everything else." He touched her hand. "God bless you," he said and headed back.

Chapter 25

"Are you certain God didn't say we should try to infiltrate the palace with our men and attempt a takeover?"

"Moto!" Zoana said sternly. "You need to concentrate on what we are doing and forget your plan. We are going in the Lord's way."

"But I don't see how it can succeed."

"I will obey God," she said, "even if I go to Getz and die. I will die for God. But I have no feeling concerning my impending death."

"Well," said Crazon, "there's every possibility that we will be arrested today. However, I'll face it with the rest."

"Why are you willing to do this for us?" he asked.

"You are still confused. We are doing this for the Lord. Our battle is not against people. We battle against the devil himself and his army. He may be a great deceiver and convince me to do his will. But men are not truly our enemies," said Zoana.

They were walking the mountain paths to Getz and had left shortly after Anam and Paluqua. Though their mountain route was shorter, because of the climbing and obstructions, they expected not to reach Getz until evening. Their band included Moto, four of his men, John Dunley, and the two Rasomite women. Mostly, they talked little, though Moto was eager to question the women on everything. He had admitted that, despite not liking a plan where they basically walked in and gave up, he would follow through on his pledge because of his word and because no one else's plans had ever worked. He said he would do his best to obey them.

"I still fear losing any of my men, though. We have sustained so many losses."

"But," Zoana told him, "you committed all your men to God, so they are no longer yours to lose if they should die. If we stay in God's will, I don't believe will happen. They will be in a much better place than we. They will fly directly into the arms of God."

"I know, but I still worry."

"If you must worry," said Crazon, "worry that the soles of your shoes will not wear out today."

He gave her a funny look, and they continued on in silence for some time. Finally, he could stand it no more.

"What did you mean about the soles of my shoes?"

Crazon laughed out loud. "Is that what you have been wondering? I told you that to get your mind off of everything else. It seems to have worked."

Moto laughed as well. "I have been walking along attempting to understand the great spiritual meaning of this."

She laughed again. "Well then you just keep trying to figure it out."

Moto and the two women were in the lead with the other men of Samta behind them. John, older and still not as agile or as strong as the others, trailed behind.

"Hey up there!" he finally called. "Are we ever going to take a break?"

Moto explained that there was a stream and waterfall just a few hundred yards ahead. After waiting for John to catch up, they proceeded to the watering spot. Finally, they could see the waterfall tumbling from a height of thirty feet directly before them, though it was still quite a distance to the spot

Moto had spoken of. They proceeded through a tight gulley which opened into a lovely meadow. The waterfall was not a great one, so it was still possible to speak in a moderate tone of voice.

"This is beautiful," said Crazon.

The falls cascaded into a gentle pool which led into a small stream. On both sides of the pool were expansive meadows. The further side was alive with dozens of types of wildflowers.

"Let's swim," suggested Crazon.

They had not had an opportunity since the day before leaving Dernay. They had gotten quite wet when the boat sank but had only dried out to an itchy saltiness. The men had shed some of their heavy dark clothing and wiped some of the soot from their faces, so they also wanted to bathe. Without further suggestion, Crazon dashed into the water and dove under, resurfacing near the opposite bank. In a few minutes, the rest of the travelers had followed her.

Zoana stood a few paces from Moto in the water, pointing her finger at him. "Moto, you have so easily changed races."

Before, darkened with soot, he and his comrades' complexion seemed very like that of the Rasomites. Now, his face clean, the washing of the water had revealed his rather pale complexion from living so much of his time in the darkness of the silver mine.

Moto glanced at his comrades and smiled. "It is true," he said. "Pray for me that my faith shall not be so easily washed away."

"I think," said Crazon, "your faith shall grow in boundless ways in the very near future."

"Crazon," Zoana said. "Shouldn't these men be anointed as we have that custom?"

"You're right. We have no flask or container, but why should that stop us. We'll do it right here."

The women briefly explained that they intended to anoint the men with water to place a blessing on them. John had done this while on Dernay, so he merely stood by and applauded as each man was doused. As each man had a handful of water sprinkled over his forehead by Zoana, Crazon spoke a blessing. Moto was first in line.

"Moto, you have suffered long and lived with great doubt. But the Lord is soon to reward your suffering, and your great doubt shall be turned into great faith. Let faithful obedience to the word of God soak deep into your heart."

As John applauded, Moto's happy grin turned into a quivering grimace. He quietly walked back to shore as they finished the ritual and went back to playing and swimming in the pool. No one had noticed how his expression had changed, except Crazon. When they had finished with the other four men, she waded ashore and sat beside the downcast man.

"Something has deeply disturbed you, my friend. The Lord says if we share our burdens with each other we can pray for each other. What is wrong?"

He was quiet for a few seconds and chewed on his lower lip as he wondered how to express what he had done. "I guess I shall just say it. I have betrayed you."

Crazon was shocked.

"Not, sweet woman, as you may think. When I learned of Zoana's plan to walk right into the palace and allow God to work, I thought it was a foolish idea. We have waited so long for this opportunity that I didn't want to waste it. I felt it would be our last chance."

"Moto, what have you done?"

"I ordered my men to gather the rest of our people and to infiltrate the palace. My order was that if we came under harm, they were to attack. If we were arrested, they are to break us free."

"Oh, Moto," Crazon whined. "How could you not trust us? How many men do you have?"

"How many can I order about? Perhaps thirty, maybe forty. However, this is to be a major offensive. It has been planned for months. I do not know how many of the palace guards or soldiers will follow us. At the moment of the attack, the entire island will erupt in civil war."

"The whole island?" She recoiled dubiously.

"In every corner we have our people planted and prepared. The palace will come under attack, and servants from Afeena here on Akadon will slay their masters. We have men prepared to free the slaves working the quarries on the north side of the island. We have even sent spies to Leetra to tell the Island Commander of our battle for victory."

"The Island Commander is one of you?"

Moto nodded. "If he is honorable to his word, he will immediately declare Leetra's independence from the emperor. There may be fights there as well."

"And on Afeena?"

"Afeena is too hard to reach. However, there is only a light guard there because there are few men on the island. As soon as our victory here is sure, we shall send John Dunley with several ships to Afeena to declare their independence."

She looked across the water to where John was playfully thrashing water at one of Moto's men. "Does John know this?"

"He knows that when we are free, he shall be sent with help to Afeena. He knows nothing of our strategy. The men with us do not know I have ordered this, either."

"Oh, Moto, so many people may die. What can be done?"

"At this point?" He threw up his hands. "It is hopeless to stop. The traps are laid all over the island. Even if one part fails, the rest may be assured. It cannot be stopped. I guess all that can be done now is to pray to God for his hand."

Crazon waved at Zoana to join them. When she arrived, Crazon explained in detail what Moto had told her. Zoana sat listening to Crazon with her face downcast and head shaking throughout. Each time Crazon added another piece and began to explain, Zoana would groan.

Finally, Zoana looked up at Moto. The three sat huddled together on the grassy slope. Moto put his hands out in resignation and sat back in fear for a stern rebuke or even a physical attack. Zoana looked back down and began praying quietly to herself. She finally looked back at Moto. She had tears in her eyes.

"Are you ready to go?" she asked them.

"But what of all the things we've discussed?" he asked nervously. "What can we do?"

"You may have fallen into Satan's trap when you did this. However, my God is greater than Satan. It is good that we know this. But like you say, there is nothing we can do to stop it. Even if we did not go to Getz and were to return to Samta, perhaps it would unravel. Perhaps it wouldn't. God has already told Crazon and me to go to Getz today. He shall have to take care of the details. In the future, so that innocent people are not slaughtered, I urge you to speak with the Lord before you choose your path. Anyway," she said as she stood up, "are we ready to go?"

They told no one else what Moto had done and were soon on the path to Getz once more.

"There it is!" Moto announced from his perch overlooking Getz as he pointed toward the palace.

"That old stone building is a palace?" Zoana asked.

"Well, that's what Coracus called it. It is several hundred years old. In the past, it was always just the capitol building or the president's headquarters. Coracus wanted a palace built, but there were no resources for such a thing. The quarry only produces gravel and shale, which they use for the roads."

It was the largest building in the city, but the Rasomites had expected a gleaming marble structure, not a dilapidated castle. The city spread out along the coast for about two miles and settled into the mountains about half a mile from the water. In the past, Getz had been a fairly important shipping port, exporting silver and gold products, as well as pearls, and importing grain and produce, mostly from Ifintim. It had boasted a huge fleet of ships that had sailed far and wide. Now, that was all gone. At the moment there were only two large ships in port. There were only five in the entire fleet. The rest had decayed or been lost due to lack of care. The only place the ships sailed anymore was to the other islands to keep everything under control. Besides the five seagoing vessels, there were about a dozen other smaller crafts that were also used around the islands.

They sat and watched the capitol building for a few minutes to ensure they were refreshed when they arrived.

"Well," said John after a bit, "the sun is going down. I think we'd best be heading out."

"Let's pray first," said Crazon. The eight all gathered in a circle and held hands. "Oh, God, this may be your moment to shine. Let no other plans stymie yours, dear Lord. Let everything come under you. Give us the strength and knowledge to stay on your path. If it is now in your will, Father, let years of oppression and anger die. I know you are against those things, Lord. If the time is now, don't let us get in the way."

"I am so angry at myself, God" said Moto when she had finished. "I am sorry for my faithlessness, and you can hold me accountable for it. Please God, though, forgive me. Don't let my foolish desires mess up your plans, God. Please, don't let harm come from my devious plot."

A few minutes later, the group was walking along a side street in the direction of the palace when their path was suddenly blocked by a band of soldiers. Only Zoana and Moto carried knives, so besides these, they were totally unarmed. The soldiers drew their swords. Moto went for his long-bladed knife, but when he realized his companions were standing motionless, he returned it to its sheath.

"Can't we approach them as you both did back on Samta?" he asked.

"Moto, it's not my intention to beat up the entire city of Getz," Zoana told him. "Settle down. Why have you drawn your swords?" she addressed the man who appeared to be in charge of this contingent. "Do we seem to be such a threat?"

"State your purpose!" he demanded.

"We wanted to visit Emperor Daga," she continued.

"Well, you don't just wander in like you're inviting yourself over for a cup of tea," he said. "Who are you?"

She extended a hand as though to shake hands with him. "Oh, I'm sorry," she said innocently. "My name is Zoana. And yours?"

"I am not here to enjoy your fellowship!" he snapped. She withdrew her hand. "Who are you and what are you trying to do? I had better get some firm answers."

"I have given you firm answers, my friend. I have answered your questions exactly." She waved her hand at the others. "Would you like to meet my friends? I don't really understand your questions."

"I've had enough!" He waved his hand toward his men. "Take this stupid woman and the rest into custody until we can extract some answers." He jabbed his finger only inches from Zoana's face. "I don't like to be messed with."

After they were all searched for weapons, two knives were taken away. Then they were led into the prison adjoining the palace. The captain over the soldiers had a discussion with the man in charge of the prison, which they easily overheard.

"Look," the impish prison guard snapped. "This place is reserved for special guests of the Emperor. There's not room in here for everyone roaming the streets. Place them under house arrest or something and guard them yourselves."

"These people do not have homes in town, and I will not allow them to wander around as they were uncooperative when apprehended. They need to be in here. It's pretty obvious these two women are part of the bunch that were arrested earlier."

"I don't care. They can't stay here."

"If you release these people and they cause any trouble, it will be on your head. So, tell me before we go that you've accepted responsibility."

"Of course I haven't accepted responsibility. They are your prisoners and I'm sending you away." The little guard had a whiney sound to his voice.

"Uh, excuse me," Crazon said getting their attention, "But, if it's just a problem of not enough cells, you don't have to give us separate cells."

They both looked at her dumbfounded that she seemed to be volunteering to be arrested.

"Yes," the captain finally asked, "how many cells do you have?"

"That's not the issue," he said, pulling his attention from the women. "The issue is that they cannot stay here."

"Put the men in one cell and these two women in the other. I know you have at least two empty cells."

The prison guard looked at Zoana and Crazon again and soaked in their physique, which very much appealed to him.

"I really shouldn't let them go," he finally said. "We've gotten in a couple others of their type today. I suppose we'll keep them. I'll need some of your help until I can get them all secured."

The men, including John, were all led to a different part of the prison and placed in a large pen. Zoana and Crazon were led down a flight of stairs into a much darker part of the prison to a separate cell. Their hands and feet were stretched out and manacled to the wall in a standing position. Soon, everyone else left.

"Are you certain," Crazon spoke from the darkness, "this is exactly where God wants us?"

"I'm sorry, sister. I knew we'd be arrested, but I didn't expect this sort of treatment."

They heard someone returning, and the door swung open as it had not been locked. The little prison guard stood in the doorway for a moment, holding a torch over his head. The women had not realized before that he was not only extremely short, but also quite ugly. Standing less than five feet in height, he gazed up at both women with a gaping mouth.

There appeared to be not a tooth in his mouth. His head was bald, and there was a crease in his skin running over his right ear. He placed the torch in a nook by the door. Despite the dank smell of the dungeon, as he approached them, his own putrid smell overcame them.

He stopped a few feet in front of Crazon and gazed at her from head to foot. "Lovely," he cackled. Then he turned and looked at Zoana. He reached out as though he were going to touch her and then withdrew his hand. "Delightful." He hopped up and down a couple of times and laughed hideously. He turned back to Crazon and placed the palm of his hand on her naked torso. Crazon felt her stomach convulsing and bit her lip to avoid giving him the pleasure of calling out. With both hands and feet chained to the wall, she was helpless to defend herself. Moving his fingers up her abdomen, he stopped before touching her breast and stood back.

"You realize," Zoana said firmly, causing him to whirl around, "you are endangering your life. The Almighty God has a covenant with us to protect us."

He cackled again. "He seems to be taking a day off today. All of you fools spouting about God are locked up in my dungeon. Besides, even God is not so stupid as to come into a place like this."

"And what of your fellow guards?"

"I'm the only one here right now. Just me and my prizes."

"I am not your prize!" Zoana snapped.

"We'll see," he said. He went back near the door, picked up a little stool that had been used when the women were first shackled, and placed it on the floor in front of Zoana. As he was considerably shorter than she, when he stood on the stool, he was face to face with her. "Yes, you are my prize. You know, it was only because of you two that I changed my mind and took you in." He laughed again. "Otherwise, you would be out in the streets with nowhere to call home." He placed one hand on Zoana's breast and embraced her neck with the other as he prepared to kiss her. Suddenly, she snapped her head forward into his face, toppling him from the stool backwards.

"I'll teach you who is in charge here!" he yelled. Running to the doorway, he took up the torch again and came back, waving the burning brand in her face. "You think I'm an ugly sight to see. I'll sear some flesh from your face and see what folks think of you then."

They heard the noise of a door slam from the top of the stairs, and he turned to go check on it. However, he never made it out the door as the room began to fill with men, Moto in the lead. The guard ran at him with his torch, not realizing Moto was armed. Moto instantly skewered him with his sword and the guard fell to the floor, dead.

"My men," Moto explained quickly, "they have come for me as I knew they would." He bent over the slain guard and began to extract the keys to release the women.

"No, Moto. No," Zoana insisted. "If you want to flee, then go. But our place is right here."

A voice called from outside the cell, "Moto, come on!"

"Go!" she repeated. "You are not doing what the Lord asked, but I understand. Go!"

Just then, John stuck his head into the doorway. "We cannot find any of the others. However, there are other cells around the palace." He realized the women were still locked up. "Aren't you coming?" he asked. surprised.

"I did not get us arrested so I could run away a few minutes later," Zoana explained. "You go with them if you want."

Moto was called for again and slowly walked out the door. John stood staring at Crazon.

"I cannot stay," he said. "If they knew who I was, they would kill me immediately. They know what I represent."

"Go with them, John." Crazon said. "John Dunley!" she called out as he disappeared from view. "I love you like a brother!"

In a few minutes, the prison was silent.

Chapter 26

Daga had totally secluded himself in his suite of rooms after the attack. He had forsaken the additional space and comfort of the suite normally occupied by the Emperor and had returned to his own quarters which were more easily secured and guarded. At all times, there were at least six palace guards about his rooms. His chamberlain would come to report upon every activity throughout the day and, therefore, he was aware of the influx of prisoners and all its related activities. Of course, though he knew Commander Ichvain had assumed responsibility for the prison, he was not aware of how the operation was being carried out. No one knew of the changes which had taken place in Mendoa since Commander Estigan's departure from Artuna. Everyone in the palace assumed order had been restored and that the loyalty and submission of Afeena and Leetra had been reestablished.

Daga was also aware of the conflict in Samta and that a guard had been murdered during a prisoner escape earlier in the palace prison. He was amazed the two female prisoners had been left behind, apparently from their own volition. Though he was interested in meeting the foreign prisoners, he was not unduly alarmed at the struggle for independence by the people of Samta. It would be normal during a change of leadership for the people to flex their muscles.

Though his heart and mind did not see an assassin in every person, he still jumped at the slightest sound for fear of

Coracus. He would have given everything to know Coracus' whereabouts.

He sat at his desk, writing, and nearly toppled the ink bottle when a low rap came at the door. The chamberlain saluted Daga, who spun around on his stool and indicated for his subordinate to have a seat.

"No need, sir," he said briskly. "Just one thing. All of these foreign prisoners have continually requested an audience with you. They are a very interesting group of people, especially the grey-skinned ones. They call themselves Rasomites. The three women are absolutely lovely, though they have a fierce streak running through them. The man, called Anam, has an absolutely massive physique. I know how you feel about body development. I am sure you would like to see him. However, I also know that it might not be the prudent thing to do with Coracus still on the loose."

"Any word on that search?" Daga asked.

"None, sir. He is like a phantom. Some of the guards say it is not truly Coracus at all, but his restless spirit."

"Ask Lanao if he thinks it was a ghost. How is the magistrate doing?"

"Still under guard at the doctor's home. He goes for a short walk at night with a guard and the doctor, as the doctor insists that he needs the exercise."

Daga nodded. "That's fine. He's not a prisoner. He tried to warn me, and I scoffed at him."

"Consider visiting with one of these people," the chamberlain said as he backed toward the door. "They are very bold in their tongue and speak of strange gods, though I have yet to catch them in any falsehood. Actually, they claim there is but one God and he gives them great protection."

Daga smiled for a change. "If he is a great protector, then why are they prisoners in my palace?"

"All four of the Rasomites actually had ample opportunity to leave under various circumstances. They don't act like prisoners. I might caution you, sir, that you are also a prisoner." Daga's smile turned into a scowl. "I am sorry. I did not mean to offend. If there is nothing else, I request permission to retire for the evening."

Daga nodded and the chamberlain let himself out. The guard secured the door.

"I believe I shall go to bed, as well. Not that your company isn't absolutely charming," Daga told the guard sarcastically. "But I am weary from all the activity."

He changed into a sleeping gown without calling for a servant and pulled the covers back from the bed. A slip of paper was revealed when he did so. Daga brushed it aside without thinking and sat on the edge of the bed. Then he picked up the piece of paper. On it was scrawled one word, 'DECEIT'.

"Guard! What is the meaning of this?" he demanded, waving the note in the air.

"I don't know, sir. What is it?" the guard asked as he finished turning down the kerosene lantern near the bed.

"Confess it! You placed this paper here with this damnable word under the covers."

"I cannot confess it, sir. I have not seen this before."

"You know full well that only you and I have been in these rooms. Only the chamberlain has been in since I drew these back up at noontime. If you did not place this here, then who did?"

The guard nervously attempted to deny any knowledge again when they heard a hoarse laugh in the next room and what sounded like a door slamming shut. The guard instantly ran to investigate the source. Daga nervously followed him at a distance, not wanting to be left alone.

The room the sound had come from was a tiny room with a cot in it to be used by a guard or overnight visitor. All of the walls, floor, and ceiling had been thoroughly searched by his experts for any trap doors or even the smallest crack.

"Someone was in here!" Daga snapped.

"Yes, sir. Someone was in here, but there seems to be no sign of any trap doors." He was running his hands over the walls. He moved the cot so he could search under that. There were no cabinets or any other doors in the room as it was a simple little room with a stone floor and ceiling and paneled walls.

"What do you want me to do, sir?" the guard asked, standing at attention.

"Knock down the walls!"

The guard went to the door and solicited more help, explaining what had happened. Within a couple minutes, the palace was being searched, a heavy guard put in place all around while two men arrived with huge hammers and crowbars to begin breaking down the wall in the small sleeping room. However, no one had seen anything of Coracus. His appearance and disappearance were a mystery.

Within a few minutes, the heavy paneling had been obliterated. Unfortunately, all that stood in place now were four stone walls. Try as they might, none of the people could budge any of the huge stones.

"What do you want us to do, sir?" the chamberlain asked in exasperation. "The guards are becoming more convinced than ever that this is a phantom."

"I don't know!" Daga screamed in anger. Then more quietly, he added, "I am totally open for suggestions."

"I shall double the guard. It shall tax our resources, but your peace of mind is all that matters. I do not understand. If

Coracus lives, why does he not simply come forward and assert himself. Why does he do these things?"

"Because," Daga snarled through clenched teeth, "he first wants to drive me insane. He isn't interested in being emperor, nor is he concerned for the Isles. He only wants control over people's minds. This is what I will do."

"Yes, sir."

"Whoever can find and trap and slay this rat, I shall give a choice as island commander over either island, Leetra or Afeena. Their choice."

"Is this wise, sir? The men there have served well."

"It is my decision to make who governs the islands. Commander Borda is a fat fool. Ichvain is too conniving. Let it be known throughout the Isles. I don't care if it's the lowliest milkmaid who succeeds. They shall be so promoted. You must understand, Coracus has turned himself into a renegade and assassin. He killed that young guard at the prison. He is most likely responsible for the deaths of those soldiers on Leetra. He tried to kill the warden, and now he is after me. Perhaps, you will be next. He is a criminal."

"As you wish, your majesty. It shall be published throughout the Isles immediately. Is there anything else?"

"Yes, I want to see that Rasomite. The man. What did you call him?"

"Anam, sir. His name is Anam."

"Bring this person to my quarters at once."

A few minutes later, Anam was led into Daga's quarters. His hands and feet were all shackled together, and he was escorted by two guards.

"This is too much," Daga said. "Why is he so shackled? It looks very uncomfortable. Keep his hands shackled and remove all the rest. And I don't need these extra guards. You both wait in the corridor." They removed most of the shackles, and the extra guards left the room. Daga looked at Anam and motioned to a chair. "Please, sit down." Looking toward the other two guards, he said, "One of you get us some wine." Both he and Anam settled into their chairs. "Sometimes, especially late at night, a glass of wine can be very conducive to a conversation."

"I have wanted this conversation since we first arrived in the Isles."

"I have heard it said but tell me why you came here."

"Our people and the Denarites have been sharing our lives in Ifintim for the past year. It seemed only natural to attempt to reestablish the fellowship that has always existed between the nations."

"Then those horrid creatures, the Onoshe, have been destroyed?"

"They left the valley. We don't know for certain where they went."

"So," Daga said as he cocked his head to one side, "you came here out of a mere curiosity to see if we could once again trade and such?"

"I believe you know our mission was graver than that. We had heard the people here had a very disagreeable life. We had hoped to improve their situation."

"I have heard some of this talk about your God. Do you believe we should get our joy in life from the situation we are in or should our joy come from a deeper place inside of us?"

"True joy is a gift from God. However, from what I hear, this type of joy or any type of happiness is very much discouraged here. Our goal is to lead many to God and help them find true joy and improve their situation, as well."

"And how do you expect to do that?"

"Well, let's consider yourself for example. I don't believe you've been experiencing much joy. You are the Emperor over the Isles, and yet, you live in fear."

"What would you know, sitting there in shackles, how I live?" Daga snapped at him.

"I know you fear the man you tried to kill and you called me up here in the middle of the night either to console you or, at least, to entertain you away from your problems."

"I could have you executed for that accusation. My man was right. For a man in chains, your words are very brash. So, what can you do to make me feel more joyful?"

"I can do nothing unless you are willing to repent of all your sins and reach out to God Almighty."

"But what if all I want is some joy and nothing more? I can do without God."

"Until you are willing to give something to God, he cannot give anything to you. But he will give you much more in return."

"This is all just bantering. My chamberlain said this would be entertaining."

"Sorry to disappoint you."

"Is that woman you came in with any more entertaining than you? Perhaps, I should have sent for her."

"I'm afraid her talk would be much like mine. Until we have some common ground, none of us are very entertaining."

"Guard! This one can go back!"

One of the guards opened the door so Anam could be escorted back.

Anam stood up. "One more thing, sir. God has revealed something to me to tell you. Earlier tonight, Coracus was in your room. You and your men searched in vain to find his way in. If you stand in the doorway to the guest room, step off three paces and face left, you will see a large stone block that looks very much like all the others. Of course, you won't be able to move it. As you know, all of these stones are block -shaped and could only be moved by several men. However, the block you will be looking at is only a couple of inches thick. It is supported by two iron posts inside. It can only be opened properly from the other side. Take a heavy hammer and knock out the block. You will then gain access to Cora- cus' labyrinth of passages, which even encircle this room."

"How can you know this? You've never been here be- fore," he asked in amazement.

"I've never even seen the room, sir, except in a vision." He was standing with the guards. "Tonight, you shall sleep well."

Daga sat quietly, considering what Anam had said about the secret entrance after he'd left. After a couple minutes, he sent one of his guards to find the chamberlain and a heavy hammer. The chamberlain arrived with a workman a few minutes later, and Daga explained what Anam had told him from his vision.

"We have nothing to lose and much to gain, Excellency." He ordered his assistant to remove the appropriate stone block.

Sure enough, it was exactly as Anam had explained. The stone was thick enough that it would not sound hollow if rapped upon, but thin enough that by removing the two iron posts supporting it from behind, one could fairly easily slide it out of place. Beyond the now gaping hole was a small, dark passageway.

"Do you want this searched out now, sir?" the chamber- lain asked.

"No, seal up this thing for now. I am so weary I am beside myself. Place a guard in this room, and when it's light, perhaps it will be clearer. I am so tired," he whined.

"I understand, sir."

A third guard was appointed to maintain a vigil in the small sleeping quarters, which was now strewn with slivers of paneling and pieces of stone.

"How do you suppose this Rasomite knew?" the chamberlain asked.

"He said it was a vision from his God."

"Yes, but perhaps he knew because Coracus himself weaseled his way into the prison and told him. Could it be they are in league with each other?"

"I don't believe so. It would be inconsistent with everything else these people have said and done. I don't like them, but they've said not a word to cause me to believe they approve of Coracus above myself. Also, why would Coracus wish to betray his secrets to anyone? Now, I'm going back to bed. I've had enough for one night."

Late the next morning, Daga suddenly sat up in bed. The guard, who had only just come on duty, was standing at a loose attention.

The guard snapped to attention and smiled when he saw the Emperor seemed to be in good spirits. "Good morning, sir!" He saluted him. "Did you sleep well?"

"I have had the most lovely and restful night of sleep I can remember for a long time. I feel so refreshed. What time is it?"

"It is nearly lunchtime."

Daga climbed quickly out of bed. "Give me your sword."

The guard handed Daga his sword and stood back as he began dueling with the air. The second guard was seated in a chair by the door and watched the activity.

"Come at me!" Daga challenged, holding the sword high.

"But, sir," he protested as he stood up, "you are still in your dressing gown."

"Never mind that, just come at me."

The guard slowly withdrew his sword and meekly waved it about in defense of Daga's fairly heavy assault. There came a knock at the door and the guard was momentarily distracted. Daga snatched the sword from his opponent's hand with the point of his sword and sent it flying through the air. In so doing, he also sliced into the man's thumb. The sword crashed into a flowerpot, drenching the stand upon which it stood with its contents.

"Oh, my, look what I've done," Daga said. He quickly reached into his closet and pulled out a handkerchief, handing it to the guard. The visitor rapped on the door again, harder than at first. "Can you wait?" he snapped. Then Daga himself opened the door.

"Good morning, your Excellency!" said the chamberlain. "Why didn't the guard open the door?"

"Well," said Daga timidly, "he was injured in battle."

The chamberlain entered and took in the scene at a glance. "What has happened?" he asked in alarm.

"It's okay, sir," the guard said, holding Daga's kerchief over his bleeding thumb. "The emperor was just having a little fun, and I wasn't paying attention."

Daga stooped down and began picking up the broken shards of pottery.

"Your Majesty," the chamberlain said, "I'll get a servant to clean this up. You could cut yourself."

"It would only serve me right," he said as he stood up and wiped his hands on his gown.

"I trust you slept well."

"I slept marvelously," he said. "The best ever. I feel so refreshed."

"I suppose you'll want to get dressed and have something to eat?"

"Yes. Yes, of course. Send a servant to help me pick out some clothes and have something sent to the veranda. This morning I want to eat with the woman who arrived with the man I spoke with last night. What is her name?"

"I believe she said her name is Paluqua, sir. However, would it be wise to dine outside with this danger still hanging over you?"

"I don't give much of a damn about that anymore. I am certain that he is not the only person in the Isles who would like to slit my throat. I'll eat on the veranda. See that the prisoner has the opportunity to clean up and give her some fresh clothing, if she wants. You really must do something about that smelly, old prison."

"Of course, sir."

Later, after Daga had bathed and was dressed, he sat on the veranda outside his quarters. The doorway into his quarters had previously been sealed shut, but the seal was now broken. There were several palace guards patrolling the area as he sat and sipped his tea. The chamberlain arrived with Paluqua, in bonds, and two guards. Daga stood as they approached him.

"How can she enjoy this lovely meal we've prepared all laced up like that? Let her go. I am certain if she truly wanted me dead or she wanted to flee, she could do so with the nod of her head."

Once free, Daga took her by the hand and led her to the table laden with fruit, cheese, and breads.

"We have two different teas this morning. One is just the regular blend that folks all over the islands have available. However, the other is a special blend I had made specifically for myself." Paluqua sat down as Daga picked up the pot with his own tea in it.

"I am truly flattered by this generous offer of yours, sir. However, it is difficult for me to party while my loved ones are still in chains and go hungry."

Daga looked at his chamberlain. "Why are they being treated so rudely?"

The chamberlain nervously gesticulated. "They are prisoners, your Majesty."

"Fine, they are prisoners. Keep them locked up, but not in fetters, and see that they get adequate rations." The chamberlain nodded his head. "Perhaps you don't understand what we're dealing with here."

"I'm afraid I do not, Excellency." Daga stared at him for a few moments. "Could you explain, sir?"

"No, now that I think about it, I cannot explain because I don't know either. Therefore, it is best that we proceed with discretion. Now, carry out my order."

The chamberlain left and Daga again lifted his pot of tea near Paluqua.

"I think I'll have the regular sort of tea, your Majesty." Daga looked a bit stunned. "Then, I can more easily drink some of your own and know its fine taste." Daga smiled and poured them both some tea from the other pot.

"I notice that you have foregone the chance to exchange your clothes for fresh garments. That is fine as you have a very, umm, nice outfit."

"We dress this way as this is our custom, sir."

"You know I spoke briefly with your man last night." Paluqua nodded as she sipped her tea. "At the time he seemed a very boring sort of person. However, as time has gone by, I have found him extremely intriguing. He said some things that just amazed me."

"Anam is a very amazing man."

Noticing she was not eating, Daga loaded his plate down with a sampling of nearly everything available and, then, switched plates with her.

"Why, thank you, sir. Why the sudden change of heart? I had heard…"

"That I was evil, conniving, slanderous? That I made a kinder enemy than friend?"

"I had heard some things."

"Let me tell you my story. As a young man, I made a significant error. I befriended a very evil person, as I was also bent toward. We spent our lives in league as we constantly attempted to get an advantage over others. Deceit and blood followed our paths. Then came the greatest deceit, to destroy my own partner. This has come down upon me like a mountain of rocks. I did it for evil gain, but I had no more than accomplished the deed and then I grew bored of my evil. I had just about decided to follow a better path, a kinder path, with more liberty than my predecessor. I found the trap had sprung on me. I became nearly mad because of my fear of him. Then, I spent a few minutes with your man, Anam. I grew perturbed and sent him away. Now, I am merely a bit confused." He stopped for a moment. "Why am I telling you all of this?"

"Perhaps," she said as she held her teacup out, "because you know it is time to repent of all your evil and come to God. I think I would like to try the better tea now."

Daga nervously motioned to a servant to pour them both another cup of tea. "Yes. Yes, I suppose. Your Anam said things like that. He was a nice person, but you are far more fetching than he. Though I would like to trade him for those beautiful muscles."

"Don't you see, Daga. It is not the outward flesh that matters, but what God sees on the inside." She took a bite of fruit and sipped her tea. "Yes, this is ever so much better than the other. What do you say? Do you want to settle for the old, regular blend concerning your life? Or would you prefer the special blend that the Lord himself has prepared?"

"It is easy for you to say. You are young and lovely. But me, I have spent my time. I am old. I cannot go back and change the past, and the future is so short."

She shook her head. "The future is forever, and it can start right now. You said yourself you would like to begin anew. Wouldn't it be easier with God himself at your side?"

He sat quietly for a minute. "What you say may be true. I will consider it. Please, stay and eat." He stood up. "There are matters I need to attend to. When you are done, the guard will take you back." He turned and nervously walked into his suite.

"How is the exploration going?" he asked as he approached a guard supervising several men preparing to go into Coracus' secret passageway.

"They're just beginning, sir. There are four men already inside somewhere. The rest will move out in a couple of minutes. I went in myself first and only proceeded a few feet. There are several side routes."

"Who created all this? Was this something of the president's construction?"

"No, sir. These chutes seem to be as old as the building itself. So, whoever designed them is long gone."

"To think that Coracus knew of these passages and never let me in on it. Perhaps we were both less than thorough with each other."

As they spoke, two of the other men entered the dark hole. They each carried lanterns and dressed light.

"I notice they carry no weapons."

"That was a hard one to convince. However, I reasoned that anyone who might be in there would be scared off and that our people needed to be agile enough to get through tight spots."

"Keep up the good work and let me know if you discover anything of interest."

"Yes, sir!"

Daga went back onto the veranda to discover that Paluqua and most of his guards had left. The servants were cleaning up the meal and snacking from different plates. When they saw Daga, they recovered themselves and apologized.

"Eat all you want," he said surprising them. "No sense having a waste. But, bring my tea into my room." A sudden depression came upon him and he despondently lowered his head, returning to his room to write.

Chapter 27

"The trap has been sprung, Moto. A message has been sent to Ichvain. We may be victorious without even a battle at the quarry as there are so many prisoners and so few guards. The message has percolated throughout Akadon that it is time to strike. As soon as we attack, the whole island will go into an uproar."

Moto had gathered a few of his men in a bar to find out what had taken place since he had been arrested and spent a night in hiding. He had hidden out with the others who had been caught, including John Dunley, in a basement over-night. The bar they were in was still closed, so it provided some security for this meeting.

"Is there no way to reverse this?" Moto asked.

"Reverse it?" one of them snapped. "Why on earth would we want to do that? If it were even possible."

"I feel I have betrayed our new friends. We agreed to follow them and then reneged. If only there were a way."

"I agree with what you say," said one, "but you gave us the order yourself. We follow you. It is like feathers in the wind now. There's no way to cancel the order. What if we did so and some did not get the word? This would not only jeopardize the revolution but would put many in death's path."

"I agree," said another. "We've plotted this for a long time. We have friends in high places. Our enemies are becoming weak and confused. Now is the time to strike."

"When it was conceived," said another, "you said it was an excellent plan. Now, with Coracus out of the picture and Daga acting weak, it is even better."

"Sir," said the first, "we need your support. Anything less than total commitment will cause our support among Daga's troops to wander. We cannot risk it."

"Fine then," Moto said, taking a deep breath, "let's go do it."

Chapter 28

"Tell the two Rasomite women I have yet to talk with that I wish an audience with them in court," Daga explained to the chamberlain.

"In court, sir? Would that be wise?"

"All my life I have tried to use discretion. Now, I discover I don't even know what the word means. Have them sent for. I'll meet them in my royal robe."

"What do you suppose is going on out there, sister?" Crazon asked Zoana.

"I wish I knew for sure. I guess we'll just have to have faith in God. I suppose Moto is organizing some sort of final conflict."

"That's really going to mess things up for witnessing to the Emperor."

"God has a plan. I've never seen it fall together just the way I'd wanted."

Due to Paluqua's request, they had been unchained and moved to a nicer cell. This one had a hardwood floor, table, chairs, and cots to rest on. They'd also been given a satisfactory meal. However, they still had no contact with anyone except for a couple of guards who knew nothing. The guards were friendly, though, and had quietly listened to and were considering their witness.

"Crazon, let's pray."

They came together and prayed for an opportunity to speak to Daga. They also prayed for all their friends who were locked up. They prayed for Moto and John Dunley and as many of the people from Samta as they could remember. They finally began naming and praying for people left behind in Ifintim. They heard a noise at the cell door and three guards entered the cell.

"Emperor Daga wishes your attendance before him in court," said the one. "Before your appearance you will be allowed the luxury of bathing and be offered fresh clothing."

"The bath would be appreciated," Zoana said. "However, we won't be needing any new garments as we are quite used to our own."

A few minutes later, they stood unshackled in the Emperor's courtroom under heavy guard.

A warning cry was sounded without. "Emperor Daga! All silence!" All the guards quickly fell into formation, and the room became suddenly quiet. Daga entered from the side with his chamberlain and slowly proceeded to his throne. Daga scanned the room and then returned his vision to the two Rasomite women. Before this, his face seemed set in seriousness, but a moment after letting his eyes come to light on the women, a smile appeared. Daga waved his hand for them to come forward, and they did so.

"It's with great pleasure that I've arranged this meeting," he said. "I have spoken with your friends, the other two Rasomites, and though their words cut my heart, I have enjoyed our brief time together. But I know they have, as do you, so much more to tell me."

There was in the courtroom directly opposite the throne and above the main entryway, a huge carving of wood consisting of a series of spiraling grapevines which formed a series of sweeping circles. There was a sound like two pieces of wood slapping together, and the wooden carving fell to the floor. Behind this now open porthole sat a shrouded figure with a bow. He yelled out one word in his hoarse voice, "Deceiver!" and let fly an arrow. As the arrow sank into Daga's chest, the assassin vanished.

Zoana, who was closest to the Emperor, except for the chamberlain who ran and cowered behind an arm of the throne, was instantly at Daga's side. When he was struck, he slumped over and fell to the floor. Zoana stooped onto the floor, cradling the dying Emperor's head in her lap.

"Oh, woman of God," he strained to say, "everything is empty and foolish. I had wanted to know more of your God. Now, it is too late. I fear I shall plunge into the evil hands of the other god."

"There is time," she whispered. "Repent of your sins and reach out to the Lord."

"I do repent. I truly want to be with your God." He was barely breathing but rallied again. "I would have traded all that I ever had for one day alone with such as you." Then, he was dead.

As soon as the arrow flew, there was a flurry of activity. When the chamberlain realized the assassin was gone, he quickly recovered his composure and leapt to Daga's side, standing over them both. However, suddenly, the palace guards seemed to be battling amongst themselves. Moto appeared at Zoana's side, wearing the uniform of a palace guard.

"Are you responsible for this crime?" she snapped at him.

"I would have. I am not. The assassin was Coracus himself. He still lives."

Suddenly, the chamberlain pulled his own sword and challenged Moto. Zoana stood up and looked around, realizing many of the palace guards were actually Moto's men, and the entire courtroom had turned into a melee. One of them flung open the main doors and the room became crowded with men of both factions. Many already lay dying.

Moto's handful of men were becoming hopelessly outnumbered as more palace guards and soldiers continued to arrive. One could not hear a voice due to the clatter of nearly a hundred swords. Zoana attempted to reason with the chamberlain to restore order as Crazon had sunk to her knees in the midst of the battle in prayer.

Zoana, frustrated with her wasted efforts to speak reason, snatched a sword from a slain palace guard and attempted to interpose herself between Moto and the chamberlain. She was, unfortunately, also drawn into the fight when several guards drew her off from the others.

One of Moto's men was engaged with a guard near where Crazon was still stooped in prayer. She paid little attention until suddenly the guard thrust his sword into his opponent's neck and the man tumbled against her. Crazon looked hard at the man before she recognized him. The dark shroud had been replaced with the uniform of a palace guard. The soot had been washed away from his face. He gazed into Crazon's eyes with the countenance of a man that had lost his last battle.

"Geen," she cooed into his ear as she sidled alongside him. "Not you too?"

"I am fallen, Crazon," he mumbled through parched lips. Blood spewed from his neck where he had been pierced and from his mouth as he spoke. "I have failed you and God. Is there no hope...?" He had to stop speaking as he was choking on blood. "I had told you I had but one thing yet to give. Now they have taken that as well. There is no hope for me now."

"There is hope," she said, weeping. "Remember the words of repentance and remember, especially, how much God loves you." He nodded his head slightly. "Pray for repentance and also if the Lord may spare you."

"I am sorry, Lord. God help me!" he screamed out and died in her arms.

Despite the heavy casualties, it seemed as though Moto's men would not surrender. They were certain that to surrender would be to die. They preferred to die with valor. The chamberlain and Moto continued to engage. Though most of Moto's men were battling with at least two or three guards, everyone had let them battle alone from respect. Moto released a blow to the side of the chamberlain's face which nearly toppled him but caused no damage. He recovered his position and charged at Moto, thrusting his blade into his opponent's ribs. Moto slumped against a wall. The chamberlain, believing the battle was over, stepped back and lowered his sword.

Moto suddenly regained his strength and rammed the chamberlain through his belly with his sword. As the man fell to his knees and dropped his sword, Moto again stabbed him in the chest. The chamberlain crumbled to the floor, convulsed a few times and lay still.

Then, his strength gone and the pain so intense he could no longer stand, Moto fell to his knees and dropped his sword. When the handful of his troops that were left saw Moto fall to the floor, their minds were quickly sapped of their desire to fight. Zoana threw her sword aside and again ordered everyone to drop their arms.

It would have been hopeless to continue. Moto had begun his battle with an advantage of twenty-four men, including himself. Only six remained standing. The rest lay dead or wounded. There were at least fifty palace guards and soldiers still prepared to engage, though they had suffered more losses than their opponents.

The Captain of the Guard quickly took control.

"You must surrender! Your battle is hopeless! You cannot hope to succeed with these odds. Now quickly, throw down your arms!"

Moto's men all glanced about and with great fear and trembling dropped their weapons. They were immediately arrested and led away. Palace servants began to arrive to tend the wounded and, showing compassion, tended the injured from both parties without respect to persons. Zoana and Crazon were also led away with the six other prisoners.

As there were no guards at the gates or outer doors, the arrival of visitors on the scene of battle was a great surprise. Everyone's attention was turned to the three well-dressed ambassadors. The room became hushed. Acton and Climus escorted Marcis, still using a walking stick, a few paces into the carnage. The Captain of the Guard, who had been accompanying the prisoners, approached them and stopped several paces away.

"Acton! Climus! Your timing for a visit is not well. As you can see, a revolt has been subdued here. Your father, Lanao, is residing with the doctor, Shapel. I suggest you go there until you are summoned." He started to turn away.

Suddenly, Zoana and Crazon realized the third man was Marcis, whom they had supposed dead.

"Marcis!" Zoana called out. "You're still alive! Oh, praise God!"

"Very alive. Release these women immediately!" he ordered the captain.

"What is the meaning of this?" he demanded. "These women were accomplices in this failed attempt at an overthrow."

"These women are citizens of Ifintim of which I am ambassador."

The captain smiled. "What is that to us? We have more people in this very courtroom than you have in all the city of Ifintim."

Climus stepped forward. "We all came as ambassadors. Ifintim and Leetra have signed an alliance. We have also made certain trade agreements. When Ifintim is challenged, Leetra is on guard."

"You have no business doing such things as you are still subject to Akadon."

"No longer," said Acton. "Commander Ichvain has declared our independence. We are an independent country now. All assets on the island of Leetra and in its coastal waters have been appropriated. You obviously have no leader. It would be a foolish idea to assert yourself and try to live under the old ways. We are prepared to attack to defend our honor and free our people if needed. However, we prefer to go to that higher authority which has created this situation. You are outmaneuvered. Release the women!"

As if on cue, a crowd of soldiers began to form outside the entryway. Acton explained. "We have two shiploads of soldiers and volunteers, including both men and women, who are here to receive what rightfully belongs to us. We shall do so peacefully or not. I say again, you are outmaneuvered. Release the women!"

The captain nodded his head to let them go. Crazon dashed to Marcis and hugged him. Zoana, however, headed for Moto. He lay on the floor being nursed by a young girl.

"This one is still alive, miss," said the girl as she moved aside for Zoana.

Moto, gritting his teeth in pain, sat up. "You are right," he said. "God can use any situation. I am responsible for this slaughter. However, it seems, your friend and our spies have arrived at just the right moment. God is still in charge."

"He is still in charge," she said as she sat next to him. "You need to understand that and draw close to him."

Crazon had been speaking with Marcis, and he informed the captain that he must also release the other prisoners from Ifintim. A guard was begrudgingly dispatched.

"Moto," Zoana asked, "where is John Dunley?"

"I don't know. He adamantly refused to participate in this battle. He is still in Getz, I'm sure, but I don't know where."

Two other men, villagers from Samta, arrived seeking Moto.

"Sir, the prisoners on the north side of the island are free. There is no transportation, and many are still too weak to walk. But they hope to return home soon."

"How many deaths?" Moto braced himself for the answer.

"There were no deaths in the recapture at the quarry. The few guards surrendered almost immediately. However, the condition of the prisoners is much worse than we'd hoped." The one speaking looked at Zoana. "Nearly a thousand men and boys have been trapped in there. There are fewer than two hundred now to free and many are weak and sickly."

"We should go there as soon as possible to help," Zoana reassured him.

He nodded. "They are in good spirits, though, considering everything. All they desire now is to return home."

"And the house servants?" asked Moto. "Did the order ever get passed to them? Were there many deaths?"

"Deaths, sir? That was not the order. Geen himself passed that order and said you wanted no massacre. The servants were to flee into the mountains and wait until this thing was over. Many have done so. I am not aware of any deaths. He told us you had changed the original order. Did you not?"

Moto shook his head. "No, I never changed the order. I must thank Geen."

Zoana placed a hand on his shoulder. "Moto, Geen is dead. He died in Crazon's arms during the battle."

Moto's tears began to flow. "I was so stupid. I should have let someone like Geen take charge."

"Zoana!" a familiar voice called from across the room. She quickly looked over her shoulder toward Mashua and the rest of her friends.

"Mashua!" she called as she leapt to her feet and ran to him.

As they enfolded each other in their arms amidst tears, Crazon and Marcis also joined the group. Most of them had not seen each other for several days, so many tears and much laughter were spread around. Everyone would have long stories to tell, but now they merely rejoiced in the mutual presence.

"So, everyone is accounted for." said Crazon. "But what could have happened to John Dunley? I should have thought he would be here by now."

A few hundred yards from the palace, Coracus glanced around to ensure he was not followed and ducked into an alcove. What had happened at the palace had caught him totally off guard. He had overheard the conversation between Daga and the new chamberlain concerning the proposed meeting with the two strange women. So, he had prepared for a meeting of his own. His plan had been to murder his deceiving friend, allow a moment of outcry, and then produce himself to reclaim his throne. Thereafter, would follow another purging of his supposed enemies. He was not certain how to deal with the Rasomites as, around any of these people from Ifintim, he felt powerless and was careful to avoid them. However, he figured he would somehow crush this opposition after he was safely back in power. What had surprised him was the sudden reappearance of Moto and his men, masquerading as palace guards. It was because of the women, however, that he had fled. Now, he considered what to do next.

He heard a noise of someone passing by on the sidewalk, but as it grew silent again, he ignored it.

"I am looking for a pig!" someone called out, "And it seems I can smell one here."

Coracus felt he recognized the voice as someone from the past but remained in his hiding place. Then, he saw a figure creep slowly and cautiously passed him, searching as he moved. He immediately recognized the stranger as a man he had thought drowned at sea. As soon as John had passed him, Coracus silently slid his knife from its sheath. Holding his breath, he sprang from behind, encircling John with his left arm and holding the knife to his throat.

"I had thought," hissed Coracus, "that this rat had drowned at sea."

"It seems the Lord has saved both of us from a watery grave," John said. "He has brought us here this day, perhaps to die."

"Prepare to die, my greatest adversary."

Suddenly, John grabbed Coracus by the head and heaved him over his shoulder to the ground. As he flew through the air, he clutched his knife tightly, not willing to lose his only defense. However, his hand struck the ground first, crumpling under his chest. As he fell upon the ground, his own neck met the blade and slashed deep. He dropped the knife and rolled limply onto his back.

"I have gone down this time," he sputtered through a mouthful of blood, "at my own hand. I am destroyed by my own favorite treachery. You have finally beaten me…John Dunley."

Having heard the noise of the fight, two armed palace guards appeared on the scene. John turned and faced them, unarmed.

"I have slain your Emperor, though not me, but by his own hand. You are free to ram me through. I shall not stop you."

"Come with us!" one of the guards barked out.

The other guard stooped close to the body of Coracus and carefully verified he was dead. He looked up and nodded at the other. "He's dead. He really was a man and not an evil spirit, after all."

A messenger was dispatched to have the body removed, and the two guards silently escorted John back to the palace. Upon entering the courtroom, he was amazed at the carnage and pleased at seeing his friends set free. The guards left him alone as they spoke briefly to the Captain of the Guard, explaining what had just taken place. After a few moments of standing alone, John joined his friends who were still engaged in hugging and back-slapping. He explained to them what had happened.

The Captain of the Guard approached him with the two who had brought him in.

"What is your name, stranger?" he asked.

"You know me well. My name is John Dunley."

At the sound of his name, many of the guards stopped what they were doing and paid attention. They had all assumed John Dunley was dead at sea.

After a moment of surprise, the Captain continued. "This is a very awkward situation. However, the word of Emperor Daga, made shortly before he was murdered, is still valid. He made a proclamation earlier that this should be so. Whoever is responsible for the death of Coracus is to be rewarded the honor as commander of the island of his choice, Leetra or Afeena. As it seems, there is some dispute over Leetra's allegiance, and I am certain of your decision. You are now, without ceremony, which time has not afforded us, proclaimed to be Supreme Island Commander over the island of Afeena."

John stood in silence for a moment. "I humbly accept this offer," he said. "However, I have no right to claim the position. I will, though, soon return to my people and leave the request for leadership with them."

"Then," said the captain, "as there is no one in succession to rule over Akadon anymore. And, as we have obviously lost the war, let me, in a small display of charity, offer our every resource, especially that of transportation for the return of the prisoners and servants on Akadon to their homes."

John reached out and clenched the Captain's hand. "I accept your offer. Let us no longer desire to bind up each other in chains but let us be bound together with love and generosity. These days will be hard but let us pray for peace and restoration. More hate shall produce nothing good." They shook hands.

Chapter 29

Estella had gathered together several of the women and two of the guards in Estigan's home for a prayer meeting. Commander Estigan was still locked up, and though he was treated well and no one bore him a grudge, he still vehemently lashed out at the change which had taken place. Everyone in the village of Mendoa had reached out, except for him, and found the Lord. Though their outward circumstances had not changed, the village was infused with an entirely different attitude. Friendliness and concern for each other now ruled. But the women felt that a great barrier had been burst and everything would be better from then on. They felt a little naïve in their positive attitudes, but their main concern was to obey God. They did not know for certain what the future held. There had been no contact with anyone outside the village since Estigan's return.

Estella would have preferred to have met in the meadow outside of town where they had been meeting. However, the sky was overcast, and rain was threatening. As Estigan's house afforded the most room, they had gathered there. There had been singing and individual testimonies of God's work, but just as Estella was prepared to begin teaching, an excited pounding came upon the door and a young neighbor lady dashed in, tears streaming down her face.

"It's the men!" she screamed. "The prisoners from Akadon are coming." She stood trembling near the doorway for a moment and then ran back outside, leaving the door ajar.

Everyone nervously glanced at each other before the news sunk in. There was a mad dash to the door. Sure enough, in the distance down the road toward Artuna, a mob of men could be seen. By now, house doors throughout Mendoa were being flung open and the women began running down the road.

Estella was also caught up in the mad rush, and upon reaching the group of roughly forty men and boys, eagerly looked for any of her family. The appearance of the males was appalling. Most of them seemed like skin-shrouded skeletons. Their eyes were sunk in. What remained of their teeth hung out as their lips were dehydrated and pulled back. She recognized a few, but sadly saw none of hers. Lowering her head, she was prepared to start praying when she felt a little hand in hers and looked down.

"Peter!" she screamed as her tears began to flow.

Peter was thirteen, nearly a man, but his weak and scrawny body made him look more like a little child. His skin was well-tanned from the long hours working in the sun at the quarry. His lips were cracked and had been bleeding, and several teeth were missing. At first sight he seemed bald, but actually his head had been shorn close before leaving Akadon to treat him for lice. His arms and legs were so very thin, they would have easily broken under any pressure. However, Estella didn't completely register any of this. She only saw her beautiful son. Dropping to her knees on the gravel road, she gently hugged him as they both wept. Finally, she looked him in the face.

"Your father? Your brother?" she asked nervously.

He shook his head. "They won't be coming, Mother," he said clearly. "Father and Maurice are dead." He looked away from her, and she felt a wave of anger come upon him.

"It's okay, Peter. We have each other."

He looked back at her. "No, it's not that good. I must tell you the truth." Though he looked like a small, sickly child, his voice was firm and was beginning to sound deep like a man's. He waited a moment. "It happened long ago, right after they took us away."

"What happened, son?"

"Father betrayed us. We were all going to attempt an escape, but he turned us all in. They killed a lot of us. Beat them to death right in front of us. Maurice was one of those that died. I cursed father that day and vowed to get even. I didn't need to. God took vengeance. He died in a cave-in a week later. These things happened a lot in there. No one trusted anybody. I could only think about coming home to you or dying. I couldn't think about that place."

"Oh, Peter. I'm so sorry. But now we're back together. It will be better. But you mentioned God."

Suddenly, his whole countenance changed, and a smile crossed his lips. "These people came. They are from Ifintim. And John Dunley is still alive. They washed us and made us feel good. They fed us. Best of all, they told us about God. It's only because of these people and God we are free. I would do anything for them, but they are leaving soon."

"L...leaving?"

He nodded. "John Dunley is taking them home on one of the ships. How I would love to go with him."

Estella and Peter looked around at all the joyful reuniting. However, they also saw several who were backing off and who were not so joyful as their expectations were not fulfilled. He left her and approached a young woman standing alone. As he explained to her that her husband was still alive but could not leave Akadon just yet as he was very sick, she burst into tears of joy at the news and kissed Peter. He then began moving about and explaining to others the whereabouts of their loved ones. Unfortunately, it was mostly bad news.

Estella felt a raindrop on her arm and glanced up to see the sky had become quite dark. Quickly the group moved on to Mendoa and nearly everyone disappeared into their homes. Estella took Peter home and began to prepare for him a small meal from what she had. There came a knock at the door. Peter answered it.

"It's you" Peter called out. "I'm so glad to see you again."

Ahohiel stepped in, and Estella nearly upset her pot of soup.

"Ahohiel!"

"You know each other?" Peter asked. "He came in on the ship with us, but I didn't know you knew each other."

"Hello, Estella." He smiled. Then a note of sadness crossed his face. "I saw Regina. She told me about your husband and your other son. I am so very sorry." He placed a hand on Peter's shoulder. "But you have Peter. I know it is hard, but you still have more than many of the others. Some of them have lost all of their family."

She quietly stirred the soup. "I know." There were tears in her eyes again. "I shall learn to adjust. When I talked to the angel in jail, he warned me to be prepared."

"Umm, Estella." He approached her and took her hand. She put the lid on the pot and looked at him intently. "I cannot stay. I have to get back to the ship as John wants to leave soon. Very soon, probably in the morning, we'll head back to Ifintim." He took a deep breath. "This may not be the time, but I only have one chance to say it. I love you. I have loved you since the moment I saw you across the brook the day you found me. My heart aches for the sadness I know you must feel now, and though I know you still mourn the loss you just heard of, I only have this one chance. Come to Ifintim with me and be my wife. Peter can come and be strong there. We have a huge city and vast fields and orchards. I can give you so much there, but the best thing I'll give you is my love. Won't you come with me and start over?"

She stroked his cheek with her fingertips and felt his scrubby beard. He reached for her other hand and she stepped back, letting go of him. He stood perplexed.

"I can't Ahohiel. I just can't."

"But why?"

"Mainly because, as you say, it is too soon. I understand you have to go, but it is too soon. Also, because I look upon you as a very dear friend. It is because of you that the whole of Mendoa has found revival. And that's the other reason. I have a great work here as they need me now to help put all this nonsense and tragedy behind us. I'm sorry."

There were tears in Ahohiel's eyes. "I understand. I can't stay. They are probably waiting for me already." He blew her a kiss and backed toward the door. "I'll pray for you. And I'll pray for Peter. God bless you." He turned and ran out the door.

Peter and Estella stared at each other for a couple of seconds. She handed Peter the soup spoon, burst into tears, and ran into the other room. He stirred the soup for a minute and then went in and attempted to console his mother. Finally, remembering the stove was still burning, he went in and removed the soup from the burner., carrying the pot into the other room. Despite his cajoling, she refused to eat, so he ate nearly all of it himself. He was in the kitchen when the door opened, and Regina peeked in.

"Estella?"

Peter pointed to the other room. As soon as Regina was out of his sight, he began to pray. Estella had run out of crying and was sitting on the floor in the corner, staring out of her recently repaired window at the darkening evening sky.

"Estella, are you going to be okay?"

She looked at Regina and then back out the window. Regina stared at her for a moment and returned to the kitchen, where Peter, whispering, told her about Ahohiel. She returned to Estella and knelt beside her.

"Estella." Her weary eyes looked at Regina. "You made a mistake." There was no response. "I mean, did you pray about this? Or did you just choose the empty way to go?" Estella shrugged her shoulders and shook her head. "It's as clear to me as the sun is setting. But you know what? I bet the sun comes back in the morning. What will you do in the morning?"

"But, Regina," Estella whimpered.

"No! Listen to me. You didn't go because we need you here? Of course, we want you here. There's much to do. But, all over Mendoa are all these heavy-hearted women. Their hopes are crushed. Now, will you please tell me what you are going to give them?"

"I don't know," she said meekly. "I'm sure we'll pray."

"The kindest and most godly man I ever knew, though briefly, just said goodbye to you because you sent him away. So, you're just one of those heavy-hearted women who will sit around Mendoa and grow old. And what about Peter? Doesn't he deserve something out of this life? You told me yourself that Ahohiel was the dearest man you ever met."

"I said he was a friend."

"Yes, you did, with that faraway look in your eyes before you saw I was looking. Besides, what better man could you find than a best friend?"

"But he's gone, Regina. What difference does it make now? It's too late."

"It's never too late. Here's another thing to think about. You want to minister to these women? Maybe sometimes the best way to minister is not to sit around and talk about the problem, but to show people what they need to do. There are eligible men on the other islands. Estella, show these women if they want something good, they may have to go after it. Perhaps if they see you chasing after what you want, then they'll try a little harder."

"But, he's gone, Regina."

"Has Ifintim sank into the sea?" she demanded. "Chase him clear to his front door if you must. If Dunley's ship has gone, then wait. There'll be others." She took Estella's cheek in her hands. "Go and find him."

They stood up. Estella seemed unsure of herself, then she suddenly smiled. "Yes, of course," she spoke up. "It was God who brought us together."

"Look, you take father's horse. He doesn't need it where he is. You and Peter ride into Artuna. Leave the horse at the stables there. I'll come into Artuna tomorrow and bring him back."

An hour later, Estella and Peter stood on the dock in Artuna as they sadly gazed upon the darkened waters. Both of the ships which had been moored there earlier, unloading the men, were now gone. There were a few workers meandering around the unlit piers. An elderly man approached them.

"Can I be of any help?" he asked.

"I don't think so," she answered sadly. "I was looking for a man that came in on one of the ships and would have gone to Getz. His name is Ahohiel."

He shook his head. "Don't know him."

"Or John Dunley?" Peter suggested.

"Oh, I certainly know him. I'm working for him now. In fact, John paid me to go into Getz and bring back some medical supplies."

"When did you go there?" she asked absent-mindedly.

He smiled. "No, ma'am. I haven't left yet. I'm just waiting for the wind to change back. Probably about midnight." He pointed to a small skiff. "That's my little darling right there. Managed to keep it hid the whole time."

"Then, you're going to Getz tonight?" she asked.

"That's what I said. In another three or four hours when the wind's right."

"We absolutely must go with you," she pleaded. "I have no money. In fact, I have nothing at all to give you but God's blessing."

"Hey," he laughed, "I'll take that. It's worth more than silver and gold. I was just fixing to go to the inn for some dinner with the advance that Dunley gave me. Why don't you both come and be my guests? Then, I'll get ready to go."

Estella started crying again. "Oh, thank you. You don't know what this means to me."

The sun was just beginning to come up when the skiff's captain shook Estella and Peter awake as they pulled into the port at Getz. Estella looked up and down the pier. There were no large ships.

"Oh, my God!" she said out loud. "Could he be gone already?"

As soon as they touched shore, she flew off the boat, dragging Peter by the arm, and headed for a small group of men.

"I'm looking for the ship of Captain John Dunley!" she called out as she neared them.

One of the men approached her. "You've missed them. That ship left this morning while it was still dark. Was there something in particular you wanted?"

"I'm looking for a friend," she mumbled. "I'd hoped that he hadn't left yet. I guess he's gone back to Ifintim."

"Oh, no ma'am," he asserted. "That ship hasn't left, yet. Captain Dunley went with his new ship, The Farragon II, to Laytruce to bring the prisoners back here. Then, they'll be getting out of here to go to Ifintim. Who was it you were looking for?"

"His name is Ahohiel," she said as her eyes darted up and down the docks at the different boats.

"Oh, you must be the one." He laughed. "He's here somewhere. He's been blubbering to anyone who'll listen about lost love and this perfect woman he had to leave behind."

Suddenly, she saw him in a fishing boat a few paces down the dock. He stood dumbfounded for a moment at the end of a gangplank. Then, he headed toward her, across the plank, at a full run. Halfway across, he slipped and tumbled into the water. She stood on the pier for a moment and then dove in after him.

"I love you," she said as she threw her arms around him.

"I love you, too," he said, one arm around her waist, the other hanging onto the boat. "I love you, too." And then he kissed her.

Glossary
Major Characters and Isles

Rasomites — With skin in shades of gray, they wear loin cloths and the females wear braziers of animal hides. They are Godly, beautiful, healthy, and deadly.
- **Anam** — Leader of the Rasomites and one of the few males that survived their genocide.
- **Paluqua** — Wife of Anam.
- **Zoana** — Crazon's sister. Wife of Mashua.
- **Crazon** — Zoana's sister.

Denarites — From Ifintim City across the Sea that formerly traded with the Isles of Aboti.
- **Mashua** — Leader of Ifintim. Husband of Zoana.
- **Idiptu** — Navigator and advisor for the mission.
- **Marcis** — Not very religious yet.
- **Ahohiel** — Beloved of Estella.

Isles of Aboti:
Afeena — The first Isle visited by the Rasomites. Main town is Mendoa.
- **Commander Estigan** — Commander over his area of Isle. Has a wife and two daughters.
- **Lora** — Youngest daughter of Commander Estigan.
- **Regina** — Oldest daughter of Commander Estigan.
- **Estella Edisni** — Beloved of Ahohiel. Has a son.
- **Peter** — Estella's son.
- **Commander Borda** — Island Commander of Afeena.
- **John Dunley** — Rebel leader.

Leetra — Largest of the Isles. Main town is Laytruce.

- **Roda** — Nursed Marcis. Has daughter.
- **Shelley** — Daughter of Roda.
- **Sholl** — Prison guard and Lanao's assistant.
- **Commander Lanao** — Leetra's jail Commander. Has wife and two sons.
- **Cella** — Wife of Commander Lanao.
- **Climus** — Eldest son of Commander Lanao.
- **Acton** — Youngest son of Commander Lanao.
- **Commander Ichvain** — Island Commander of Leetra.
- **Bertrane** — Prison guard under Lanao.

Akadon — Home of the Dictator. Prison Isle.

- **Coracus** — Dictator of all the Isles.
- **Daga** — Chamberlain to Coracus.
- **Moto** — Samta leader of the silver mines.

About the Author

Larry was born in upstate New York and raised on a dairy farm. He always loved reading and writing and desired to be a writer, even from a toddler. His play involved searching for cattle in the pastures while avoiding imaginary aliens and terrorists. The Lord found him as a teenager, and he began to read the Bible and wonder why God seemed no longer to be active. Later, through personal experience and miracles, he found God was still very much active.

Larry loves to read, and his reading is wide spread. His favorite fiction writers are Ray Bradbury, Robert Howard and Nicholas Sparks. However, his constant companion is the Bible, which is also his greatest inspiration. He received his Graduate of Theology degree from the Full Gospel College in Coatesville, Pennsylvania. He retired from the United States Air Force having served during the war in Vietnam and the Persian Gulf Conflict. He currently lives in Arkansas with his wife, Yvonne, and has been married for 31 years. They have five grown children and seven grand-children.

Inspiration

The inspiration for this story arose indirectly from reading so many other books about godly people where God himself was rarely present in the story. It also arose from reading the Bible where God was normally a major player in the action. The story just came to me as I often had no idea what was going to happen next or why I was creating a situation the way it was going. Then, God would surprisingly reveal himself in the story. I pray the reader is as pleased as the writer.